Predemption – A Novel

Definition: 'Predemption' (noun) – Finding redemption from sin through a relationship with Jesus before one's life falls completely apart.

Glen Adams

Praetereo fini tempori in cello pace

'I pass at death into the peace of Heaven.'

This is a work of pure fiction. All the characters, places, organizations, and events portrayed in this work are purely products of the author's creative energy and are used in a fictitious manner.

ISBN: 978-1-7369268-0-2
First Edition c

www.glenadams.com

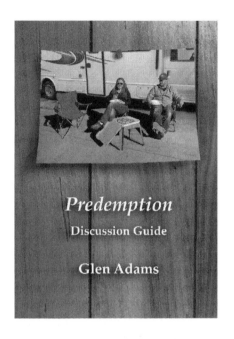

Predemption

Discussion Guide

Glen Adams

A companion discussion guide for those looking to delve deeper into the ethical, moral, and religious questions that are presented in this novel is available for purchase, in print and eBook formats.

Dedication

This book is dedicated to Jesus, the King of Kings,
and to my best friend Tammy for introducing us.

Acknowledgements

I would like to acknowledge those who
made this book a reality;

My writing posse who inspires me.

My editors Chuck Sambuchino and Cyndi Davis,
who identified many errors while providing
valuable opportunities for improvement.

Teresa and Scot for indulging me on my cover art.

And while I have been writing for years before its formation,
NanoWriMo.org is a great organization which inspires the
writer in all of us. If you desire to find motivation for putting
your own story on paper, I would highly recommend this
writing group.

You, the reader. Thank you.

Foreword

Like the American poet, Maya Angelou, who wrote that, "there is no greater agony than bearing an untold story inside you," I firmly believe that within every individual is a story yearning to be free.

Throughout human history, there have been collections of stories which feature a familiar theme, known for millennia, as the 'hero's journey'. In such stories, from Odysseus and Beowulf, to Don Quixote and Dorothy, to Skywalker and Neo, Thelma and Louise, to Bilbo and Frodo, Mulan, and even Bill and Ted, the protagonist must overcome various obstacles, in order to grow emotionally.

While *Predemption* features this aim for its protagonist, it also represents a variation on the hero's journey, known as the 'road trip'. Not only is the mission of the lead character to grow in maturity, the 'road trip' requires the hero to physically get from point A to point B in order to complete their mission. *Predemption* represents a test of both faith and fortitude.

Although *Predemption* examines a few Christian themes, this story will challenge any reader, whether or not you have a Christian background. The COVID virus isn't selective in who it infects or whose life it disrupts, and we all face similar decisions and dilemmas for dealing with this shared threat.

Can a person find God, or meaning in their life, before reaching the proverbial end of their rope? Or must they hit rock-bottom before desperation opens up the door to such a heavenly relationship or revelation? When there is nowhere to go but up, one often is in search of finding redemption. But if one has yet to find themselves fully at the bottom of the pit, spiritually and emotionally exhausted, can they find predemption?

This is my story.

1 – Flint, Michigan

Her hands ached and arms were getting tired from holding up the picket sign against the growing wind. When the city's water crisis had begun, there was a large group of angry protestors who had gathered in front of Flint city hall. There were speeches by politicians. There were entire families present, many with small children affected by the lead tainted water they unknowingly drank and bathed in. There were lawyers who pointed fingers at those in charge, who claim that they had failed to do enough to protect their constituents. News crews and reporters from all over the world descended on the scene. They were there to report on the tragedy, which had befallen the downtrodden Michigan town and its citizens who had been witness to decades of neglect and abuse at the hands of a system that had failed them repeatedly. Like its sister city of Detroit, just fifty miles to the south, it had taken every punch thrown at it, but the people were proud and kept getting back up, ready to fight another day.

Drivers that used to flow past the protestors would honk and yell out their support and encouragement as their vehicles inched their way up the main street. People who wouldn't or couldn't find the time to protest themselves would drop off food or hot coffee to those sacrificing their time for the cause. The regular visits by reporters eventually gave way to an occasional camera crew who would stop by to shoot some 'B' roll footage on the slow news days.

But even they had stopped coming by.

As with any tragedy, the fires of anger and pain and indignation could not be sustained, and interest in the city's plight quickly faded from memory. Years later, there were only two of them left manning their spot on the expansive green lawn of the city hall. It was a sad reminder that something bad must have happened here, but many wanted nothing more than to just forget and move on.

The sun was out, but it failed to chase away the chill of the unseasonably cool day. It was May, but it felt more like early March. Michigan weather always made you dress in layers and be flexible in your plans.

"I'm done," the older woman said, as she began folding up her protest sign and stowing it in one of the canvas sacks at her feet.

"Already?" Mary asked, perplexed, as she watched her friend prepare to depart.

"Not just today, Mary. I'm talking philosophically. Look around us. Nobody cares anymore. Everyone else has moved on. The entire world has moved on. We're the only two still stuck in the past. Even the guy with the walker, who used to wander by to ogle at us, has quit coming around."

Mary didn't know how to respond, their solid plan evaporating. Her own picket sign lowered slowly to the ground, free from the buffeting breeze, the tension in her arm waning. It felt good, and it felt awful. Defeat and resignation closed in.

"It was a good run. We should be proud. You and I stuck it out to the end and did some good here."

"Did we?" Mary asked. "Are things better?"

The woman shrugged. "The city changed water sources. People are checking it all the time. Water lines under the streets and running up to the houses are being replaced. They say we can bathe in it and even drink it again, so yes, I think we made a difference."

Mary nodded, still unconvinced. Her friend had three young children at home. She had been told by the lawyers that the lead that they had ingested had permanently damaged each of them, following the ill-fated change to the city's water system five years earlier, but she couldn't see a difference. There had been talks of reparations for the lifelong effects both she and her children would have to deal with eventually, but there were always promises being made, but rarely kept. Only people getting rich, Mary painfully mused, would be the lawyers.

"Besides. There's a new cause to protest," the woman continued.

Mary scoffed, knowing what she was referring to.

The novel coronavirus.

"Wouldn't every new virus be 'novel'?" Mary asked, temporarily distracted by the always present mental butterflies she had to deal with.

"I dunno. The shelter-in-place order's been lifted and the diner's opening up again. If I don't go back, the unemployment checks stop coming and they replace me with somebody else who's willing to work. Don't really have a choice, Mary. Catch-22. And I need to get ready for my shift. I just hope I don't bring the virus home and give it to the family. The kids are supposed to be alright because they're young, but mom's a different story."

Mary stood there, unsure of what to do.

Sensing the turmoil, her friend offered Mary an olive-branch. "When you figure out who we should protest against with the virus thing, call me and I'll be right back out here with you."

She smiled, but her friend couldn't see it under the flimsy paper mask that she wore. The woman could see it in her eyes, though, and smiled back. Mary moved to hug her goodbye, but her friend danced quickly back out of reach.

"No way, girlfriend. You know the rules. Six feet."

Mary watched helplessly as her friend wandered down the broken sidewalk, around a man at the curb having an animated conversation with himself, and eventually passing out of view.

"What now?"

The man at the curb, having had his own conversation interrupted, glared at her in annoyance, but said nothing.

Her answer arrived a few seconds later when the cellphone in her back pocket vibrated.

"Hello?"

"Mary, you better come quickly," the harried voice on the other end interjected.

She hung up and quickly gathered her gear, a new sense of urgency calling.

2 – Flint, Michigan

"Montana?" Mary asked, confused.

Mary's brother James, standing on the other side of the hospital bed, nodded.

She thought she had misheard him at first, but he pulled back the simple paper mask and repeated it in clear violation of the guidelines that ruled the room they were standing in. His lack of preparation and consideration made her feel absolutely overdressed. She had on disposable booties over her shoes, a long cloth gown over her upper body, an N-95 mask over most of her face, and safety glasses that she had dug out of her junk drawer at home. And she had a plastic flimsy, previously the venue of old, overhead projectors, clipped in place on the brim of her baseball cap with binder clips, which served as an ad hoc face shield.

"You're sure that's what the nurse said?" she pressed, continuing to stare down at the hospital bed where their recently deceased father was covered in a thin, white sheet smelling strongly of bleach.

He nodded more affirmatively this time. "Yup, definitely Montana." He didn't bother to pull his mask down to speak this time.

A nurse glided silently into the room, Mary noticing what she surmised to be a look of envy on the woman's face. It had been weeks since the inventories had run dry of personal protection equipment and the hospital had turned to laundering, wiping down and trying to sterilize all their gear, just to get the facility through the week. The nurse disappeared behind the translucent sheeting around the other bed in the shared room, becoming nothing more than a smudge that moved around the tight space. The patient she was checking on had tested positive only two days ago for the COVID-19 virus but had already been placed into a medically induced coma, reliant on a ventilator to do his breathing for him. Until an hour ago, that patient and their own father had been sharing a ventilator, rigged together on the fly with PVC pipe, flex tubing and duct tape, so it could serve more than one patient at a time.

Mary doubted that was something the manufacturer had ever considered. Ingenuity had once again become the name of the game when need exceeded demand. The pandemic was pushing the overwhelmed medical facilities worldwide to the breaking point. Despite being grossly overworked and underappreciated, medical professionals everywhere were still holding the line against the epidemic, even to the point of sacrificing their own lives. God bless them, she thought.

When the nurse emerged, Mary caught her eye. "Was it the virus that killed him?"

The nurse paused for a moment, looking first at the deceased and then at both of them. "We don't know," she finally admitted. "Your father wasn't here long enough to test."

"Are you going to test him now?" Mary inquired.

"Sis, c'mon. What good is that going to do?" James replied.

The nurse looked uneasy before finally answering. "We don't test if the patient has died."

"Not enough tests?" Mary asked, knowing that testing delays had led to the stay-at-home orders being issued because no one knew how extensive the infections had already spread. Despite the president assuring the country that anyone who wanted to get tested could get tested, this had never materialized. Faulty test kits followed test delays. No one truly had a handle on just how widespread the virus had gotten into the population.

"Not enough courage," the nurse admitted. "They don't even test the hospital staff. We just don't test everyone despite finally having enough kits." She looked around for anyone else within earshot before continuing. "We've been instructed to keep the numbers to 'reasonable' levels." she air-quoted the 'reasonable' part. "If we haven't confirmed that someone has the virus as part of their diagnosis and treatment, then we don't have to report it even if it's suspected."

Above the edge of the mask, Mary could see the weary and pained look in the nurse's eyes. Before the woman could continue her story, however, a doctor stepped inside the room.

"I need you both down in 528 to prep another patient for a ventilator," he ordered.

Without hesitation, the nurse nodded, turned and hustled from the room, but Mary stood her ground. When she didn't move, the doctor eyed her curiously.

"I don't work here," Mary apologized, the sheepish look lost behind all of her protective paraphernalia.

The doctor, momentarily confused, finally nodded, and then retreated.

Turning back to James and the prone form lying in the hospital bed, she thought back through all the stories and pictures from her parent's photo albums. She couldn't ever remember seeing or hearing anything about the northwest, much less the 'Big Sky Country' state. Then another thought fluttered in uninvited. "Do we even know if that's him?"

3 – Flint, Michigan

The siblings were heading for the hospital exit when a gentleman, dressed in protective gear and a mask similar to Mary's, grabbed a box from the table behind him and thrust it into her arms as she went by.

"Thank you," she said over her shoulder, trying to keep up with her brother's long stride.

"No, thank you!" the man replied through his mask, admiration apparent in his voice.

"What is it?" James asked, as Mary poked at the ends of the carton through her rubbery, oversized gloves.

"Oh, no. It's a boxed lunch. He must have thought I worked here." Mary turned, wondering if she should go back inside and explain, but the weariness and hunger convinced her otherwise.

As though reading her thoughts, her brother piped in. "Can't take it back," he speculated, snatching the bag of chips while stripping off his mask and tossing it in the trash next to him.

A bunch of folks, comprising police, fire and other, official looking people, noticed Mary emerging from the hospital and set off their sirens and began clapping and cheering. She looked around, baffled, searching for the source of gratitude, but it quickly became clear that they were acknowledging, albeit incorrectly, her departure from the facility after what they assumed had been a long and difficult shift.

This world didn't completely suck, she thought to herself, having concluded recently that its population had been cleaved almost evenly in half, one side doing what it could to stem the viral outbreak, while the other half seemed intent on setting the planet ablaze through their indifference.

Petty squabbling over official mandates meant to save lives and open up ICU wards had become the latest political, hot button. There had even been news reports of individuals throwing bleach at medical professionals out of misguided fears. It hadn't happened in their area, but Mary didn't want to take any chances by lingering too long in the hospital parking lot.

She waved at them to acknowledge that their message had been received, but noted news cameras nearby and waited before removing her mask and face shield. Someone that she knew might see the broadcast and point out that she was neither a medical professional, worthy of accepting the praise, or eating their lunches. Mary didn't need that kind of grief and misunderstanding at the moment.

"Let's go," she said, spurring James onward toward their cars.

"What now?"

"Will you go with me to spread his ashes?"

He hesitated, steps faltering, no immediate answer.

"I've never asked you for anything," she protested, to fill the silence.

Her brother raised a finger, as though to object, but his little sister wasn't having any of it.

"Taking care of the kid bullying me in second grade doesn't count, and you know it. You were five years older than he was."

James eyed her, a mix of doubt and skepticism on his face before reluctantly agreeing.

"Okay."

4 – Fenton, Michigan

Mary sat in her car and studied the distorted home through the rain dappled windshield, as a slate gray sky drifted low through the neighborhood. It could not have matched her mood more perfectly, she noted with more than a tinge of sadness.

She had been using the rain as an excuse for not having gone inside yet, but it had all but stopped coming down minutes earlier. Mary had already procrastinated coming here, to her parent's house the last few days, but the final fifty feet of the journey now seemed the hardest.

Waiting wasn't going to make any of this any easier, she concluded and stepped out, making her way onto the porch and pushing inside before she lost her nerve.

She had spent time inside her parent's house alone before but this was different, permanent she knew. Things would never be the same, and the thought pained her. She and James hadn't grown up in this house, her parents having bought the tiny place on Lake Fenton as empty nesters, but it was full of familiar family possessions and associated memories.

Their parents owned the place outright, so thankfully there was no rush to box everything up and move it somewhere else. That would all have to be sorted out later, she knew. Mary's eyes drifted around the room, landing on the kitchen wall covered in framed photographs. She stepped closer, carefully comparing each one to a memory in her head. Old photographs from before she was born. Photographs taken of the family while on vacation. School portraits and shots taken at various functions and graduations. Mary studied each one, looking for a clue where each had been taken. In all but three of the photos, she could conclusively identify the location. The rest could have been from Montana, or not. There was simply had no way of knowing for sure.

Like a private detective, Mary removed the three prints from their frames and confirmed that there were no telltale locations scribbled on the back, before reassembling and returning each to its assigned space on the wall.

Did it really matter? In the end, she concluded, it didn't. Mary had spent years of her life protesting the lead poisoning of her adopted hometown, but that was over now. The virus was spreading, but there wasn't yet a target on which she could lay blame and hold it accountable. Until that time came, however, she needed somewhere to direct her energy, a cause that Mary could champion.

Her father had made his intentions clear and although she had already coerced her brother into the idea of going to Montana, she had yet to fully commit herself to the task. That changed now, Mary knew, feeling the sudden shift in her heart. She no longer wanted to see this through, she needed to accomplish this mission. Montana or bust, Mary concluded.

She mentally set the task aside, knowing nothing else could be accomplished on it tonight. This was one of the coping mechanisms she employed at night when everything was weighing on her mind and sleep proved elusive.

Mary switched gears and began drifting through the different rooms. While she didn't have a heavy, emotional investment in the home itself, it was different for all the magical furnishings which filled the cozy, cabin-like space. Maybe not the heavy wooden coffee table on which she had split her lip, requiring stitches on her eighth birthday, but the couch from which she frequently launched herself skyward like Superman? Good times. The dining room set draped in blankets, which had served as the frame for her forts until meal time arrived? Fond memories. Mary remembered spending so much time under there with a favorite book. Priceless.

Mary could feel a familiar sense of loss and panic bubble up inside her. Tears were weighing down her eyelids. Trying to push her emotions back down inside her, she stepped into the kitchen and found the homemade spoon rack her father had made for his loving wife of nearly forty years. It was the last place she thought to look.

Gettysburg, Statue of Liberty, Boston, D.C., Kitty Hawk, St. Augustine.

Mary made her way through the collection, coming no closer to Montana than Kansas City and Hollywood. She sighed and pushed the hopeful inquiry away again.

The rest of the walls contained artwork that fit the house or her father's passion, fishing. Terry Redlin prints were spread around, always a welcomed birthday or Christmas gift if she and James could think of nothing else to get him. When Mary was younger, she had scored an awesome shadow box full of antique lures at a garage sale for five bucks, and she beamed with pride when her father had opened it. She smiled again, vividly remembering the genuine emotion that he showed when her dad had unwrapped the gift. No matter what happened to everything else here, James wasn't getting that.

A wave of sadness began pressing her, but she shook it off and continued towards the bedrooms in the back. If someone come to visit and had ventured no further than the living room, they would have concluded that her father was a simply a man who loved being outside, on a lake, rod and reel in his hand. If the visitors had reached the back bedroom, though, they might have concluded that they had intruded on a room occupied by a monk. Twin bed and nightstand, with a well-worn, leather-bound bible resting on top. Plain dresser and a single, simple lamp.

Modest by any standard, the walls were adorned with framed prints of his favorite Christian verses. A few crucifixes, chosen with great care over the years, hung on the walls. She never understood how he chose them, and sadly, she now recalled, would never ask him about his selection criteria. Mary would point some out to him, finding what she was certain would be a winner, but more often than not, he'd just shake his head and dismiss them outright without a second glance.

His favorite, she knew, was the one he had made himself from a single palm leaf they had given him at church on one Easter Sunday. Sitting in the pew, he had mindlessly folded it up into the shape of a cross during service and seemed genuinely surprised by how well it had turned out. Bringing it home, he proudly tacked it up in the bedroom above the headboard. He beamed with pride as she watched.

Bittersweet.

They had been regulars at the local, Christian non-denominational place down the street until her early teens. She had grown up having chats every day with Jesus. Some kids she had learned had had invisible friends in their lives, but not Mary. Jesus had been every bit as real to her as her own parents or brother. Nearly every day, the Lord made time to stop by and enjoy having tea with her in her fort under the dining room table. Mary cherished their time together.

But that didn't happen anymore, she remembered, a tear escaping down her cheek. Somewhere between then and now, Jesus had quit visiting. Mary searched her memory of when it might have happened or why, but came up empty.

She reached out at the sense of loss, her fingertips brushing the palm leaf crucifix above the bed. The brittle, bottom-half flaked away under her delicate touch, small pieces dusting her father's pillow. Mary felt a piece of her crumble, too.

Outstanding.

The symbolism wasn't lost on her, as the tears finally flowed. If Mary had truly believed, she should be happy knowing that her dad had been reunited with mom and that all of their pain and anguish of this world was permanently behind them. But when her mother had gotten cancer years ago, and Mary had quit attending church service, doubts crept into her head and heart.

Small cracks in Mary's faith widened into chasms as the cancer first took her mother's hair, then her dignity, and finally her life. The death had shaken Mary to the core and frankly; she didn't know where she stood on her beliefs today.

She might not have been able to recall exactly when her tea times with Jesus had ended, the faint floral aroma of her mother's favorite tea now lost on her, but she knew the exact date when she had last attended a formal church service. It had been the day her mother had lost her fight with cancer. Anger had eventually given way to apathy. She no longer just wanted to believe in God. Mary needed to believe in Him now. But time and doubt left her feeling cold and hollow inside.

Then the tears came fresh and hot and instead of trying to fight the flow, she opened up and embraced them.

5 – Fenton, Michigan

Mary awoke confused, her tired and swollen eyes struggling to focus on the cryptic view in front of her face. When she sat up and hit her head on the underside of the dining room table, the world made some sense.

Crawling out from under the blanket-draped table, it surprised her to find sunlight shining into the room. She had not planned on spending the night at her parent's house, but she hadn't felt herself in a good enough place to drive home, so that she was still there had come as no genuine surprise.

When she found her phone, several things were revealed. It was mid-morning and the appointed time for meeting James at her apartment had already passed. The other revelations were the two voicemails waiting for her.

Only one was from her brother, though, explaining that he had arrived at her place only to find her absent. He hadn't sounded overly concerned, even with her being the more responsible of the two, and was heading to their parent's house now, having correctly guessed where she might be found. The second voicemail, however, was disconcerting. The situation bringing her fully awake faster than a strong cup of dark tea and a hot shower would have accomplished.

Mary was wondering who to call first when the sounds of an enormous engine reached her ears. Peering through the front window, she could see the familiar Winnebago sitting idle at the curb. She stepped out onto the porch to greet him.

"You look rough," he commented.

She hadn't gotten a view of herself, but based on how she felt and where she had spent the night, it was probably a fair assessment.

Because of the viral outbreak, they knew it was going to be a challenge to find accommodations on the trip and places to eat. Flying, they had concluded, was not an option, given all the unknowns. James had been inspired, spending last evening getting the family RV ready for the trip. He had offered to let dad store it in his driveway over the winter, so the answer to their dilemma had literally been right in their faces the entire time.

She stepped over and gave him a hug.

"You don't look ready to go. It's time to get this road trip rolling," he said, clearly not wanting to step into the house for even a moment. He would have to overcome that hesitation eventually, but she wouldn't hold him to it until after they had returned.

"Let me grab a few things and I'll be right out."

Mary had to give him credit. This unscheduled vacation, to spread their father's ashes, had been all her idea, and despite his earlier apprehension, James seemed to be in the right spirits. After locking up the house and retrieving her bag from the trunk of her car, she wandered towards the RV.

"They can't find him," she said.

"Who?"

Mary huffed with exasperation. The answer should have been perfectly obvious.

"They can't seem to find dad. The hospital said they released the body. The funeral home confirmed they picked him up. Cremation services said they received him into their facility, they cremated him and returned him, and the funeral homes said they got him back again. But now they can't find his ashes. They haven't had anyone else picked up today, so they're confident that he has to be there somewhere and they're checking."

"How is that possible?" he asked rhetorically, his own frustration growing.

"Not sure. Everybody is overwhelmed at the moment. Bodies are stacking up and over-capacity everywhere. People don't understand how even a small increase in patients, or customers, can break the system. Everyone assumes there's an abundance of space, even though that's impractical and prohibitively expensive. They said they'd call me once they checked their records and had a look around."

James started laughing, but not in a *ha ha* sort of way. It wasn't a maniacal, mad scientist sort of laugh either. More of a deep, *I can't believe it*, kind of humorous guffaw.

"This is so like him," he practically spat. "He could never show up on time for anything."

Mary considered correcting his assumption that their father couldn't have had anything to do with the tardiness, but he was clearly hurting and they needed each other if they were going to pull this thing off. The trip had already experienced its first stumble and hadn't even cleared the starting line yet.

While James was already in the throes of coming unglued, she was strangely calm. It was probably best if they each fell apart at different times, now that they only had each

to rely on.

The phone in her hand vibrated unexpectedly,

surprising her.

"Hello?" She gave James a thumbs-up and then hung

up. "They found him. They wanted to bring him here, but I

told them we would go pick him up. I don't want to take any

more chances."

He nodded and climbed behind the wheel.

She threw her bag in the back, strapped in, and they

were off.

Twenty minutes later, James had the RV idling at the

door, the cremation society not allowing anyone inside for

safety reasons. They didn't refer to it as curb-side service,

like any open restaurant not possessing a drive-thru window,

but that's exactly what this looked like.

After calling in and confirming Mary's identity, a

solemn looking gentleman, formal-looking, black mask in its

proper position, stepped out and strolled solemnly towards

the RV. Despite the distasteful look that some folks might have conveyed upon eyeing their choice of vehicle, given the funerary circumstances, this man's poker-face betrayed nothing of the sort. After some pleasantries, he held out the beautifully stained wooden box containing her father's remains, and a crisp, properly folded flag for his military service in Korea.

"I'm sorry, we can't do more for him," he apologized smoothly, like everyone seemed to in his profession, "considering his service to our country. Thank you."

Mary nodded, hoping she was conveying the required heaviness given the occasion, despite her body wanting to scramble back in the Winnebago and get going.

While it should have been a solemn moment, heavy with pomp and circumstance, it felt more like they were picking up takeout and heading home.

The man nodded as though an acceptable amount of silence had passed and that Mary had been released from some unknown required time of mourning. The funeral official acknowledged James, still behind the wheel, with a slight bow, and then turned on his heel and walked back inside the building.

Mary paused, looking down at the items in her hands. Did protocol warrant her saying something, given that she had just taken possession of her father's physical remains? Not now, she concluded, figuring that there would be time for that at the other end of the journey. She climbed in back of the RV, but it didn't feel right to tuck 'dad' in a cupboard for the entire trip, so she belted him into the sofa and set their father's favorite Detroit Tigers caps on top of the box as though he were wearing it. Mary was tore up at the sight, but took a deep breath to keep her emotions in check. There would be plenty of time for that too at the end of the line.

She took her spot in the front passenger seat again and nodded. Her brother dropped the RV back into gear and rolled out of the empty lot, pointing the twenty-five-foot vehicle towards the freeway. Mary paused and turned.,

"Do we even know if that's him?"

6 – Durand, Michigan

"What made you think of the Winnebago?" Mary asked, after half an hour of riding in silence.

"It was available, just sitting in my driveway. Why pay for hotels?"

Mary's eyes narrowed as she studied him. "You hated this thing."

It wasn't a question, he noted.

"Times are tough. We're both laid off, wondering if our jobs will still be there when this thing blows over, you know?"

She knew. Twenty-five percent of the country was out of work and under shelter-in-place orders, with no clear idea when a new normal would settle in again.

"Just made sense since we don't know if hotels will even be open," he added.

That was a brilliant answer. Maybe her big brother was finally growing up, Mary thought.

"Besides, there's no way your car would have made it and mine is a lease that's getting up there in miles," he concluded.

"And you just ruined it," she exclaimed under her breath.

"What's that?"

"Nothing," Mary said. Then a butterfly in her brain fluttered by and the distraction took her thought process in another direction. "Handy that you had kept the RV close this winter."

He nodded, either not thinking it required an answer or choosing not to address it. He wasn't the type to pass up a compliment often, so she continued to stare at him, the silence drawing out between them. It was a tactic she often employed with James.

"Yeah, sure was handy. Right there and ready to go when we needed it," he replied, thumbs up, and eyes still squarely on the road ahead. Mary had detected the telltale change of cadence in his speech, something he couldn't avoid when he was outright lying or was hiding something.

James could be a generous man with his time and money, she knew, but it often took a nudge to get him moving in such a direction. Even in her tired state, she knew that something weird was going on but couldn't quite put her finger on the source, so she continued to stare until James finally broke and felt compelled to fill in the silence.

"I think dad has two million dollars squirreled away somewhere. Figured if he had it stored in here, it wasn't safe to leave the RV sitting unattended in a storage lot somewhere. Few large spaces, but there could be a note, or map I suppose, on where he put it, and that would be a lot harder to find."

After hearing crazy stuff from her brother over the years, him dropping a strange bombshell like that didn't seem terribly out of the ordinary. From anybody else, however, it would have blown her mind.

"Come again?" she asked, clearly wanting to know more.

"I couldn't go through the house obviously and don't know if dad has a safe deposit box, so that only left the Winnebago. Thought I better keep it close, just in case."

He looked sheepish as they exited the freeway and transitioned onto the surface streets, heading towards their first destination.

"So, dad told you he had it, but didn't say where?" Mary prodded.

"No, he didn't say anything about it."

"So, he didn't confirm to you it actually exists?"

"No." James said, with a shake of head.

"Then why do you assume he had two million dollars?"

"Because his bank balances don't show it."

Mary leaned back, both confused and amused.

"And you assume, because his bank accounts aren't flush with cash, that he must have a load of money stuffed in his mattress?"

"No, don't be silly. I've checked out his mattress," he confirmed.

"My bank accounts are pretty lean. Do you assume I have a million dollars stashed away in my lingerie drawer?"

"No, of course not."

She had to laugh at how this absurd conversation was playing out. Not the first, nor probably the last time, she surmised. With a shake of her head, Mary played this out to the end, already bored with the stopped vehicles that had them boxed in on all sides.

"Okay. I'm just trying to get a line on your thought process here," she said, noticing that the traffic ahead was stopped and that some people were abandoning their cars and trucks in the roadway and continuing on foot.

"If dad didn't tell you he had it, and you couldn't assume it, what gives you the idea it even exists?"

Her brother was checking the mirrors and traffic ahead, seemingly oblivious to her question, a common tactic of his passive-aggressive avoidance strategy.

"Well?" she nudged.

"What was the question?"

"The two million dollars of dad's missing loot?"

He had that look on his face again whenever Mary calmly and scientifically explained why one of his wild theories couldn't be valid. Doubt had filled in his features.

"I have a source that told me it exists."

"What?" she exclaimed, somewhat taken aback. His normal, outrageous claims were often nebulous, but this source was potentially something that she could logically chase down, a thread to be pulled. Not just his usual rumors and innuendo, told to him by a friend of a friend whose name he could never quite recall. "Who is this mysterious source of yours?"

The RV came to a complete stop, the traffic no long inching forward.

"Our cousin told me about it," he replied, dropping the nugget of information like it was obvious and not in need of further explanation.

"Our cousin is your source?"

James didn't reply, choosing instead to ignore her observation.

"He's ten years old," she added.

"Really? I thought he was at least fourteen," he stated, as though four years would have made a world of difference in the information's credibility. "But when you put it that way, it does sound rather far-fetched."

Mary started laughing, and thankfully, her brother joined in. It felt good to relieve some of the grief they both had been bottling up.

7 – Lansing, Michigan

When the tears of laughter cleared, she looked around and noticed three things.

One, straight ahead, the Michigan capitol building rose majestically in the distance.

Two, they were stuck in traffic next to Sparrow Hospital.

Three, there were quite a few folks decked out in hospital scrubs who were directing traffic but not getting much of a response.

Noticing people wearing scrubs coming her way, she slipped on her mask and rolled down the window. "Thank you for taking care of us, and not just during the pandemic," Mary acknowledged, waving the employee down.

The woman paused, stared at Mary for a moment, and then warily stepped towards the RV. "You're not here for the protest, are you?"

"Protest?" Mary asked, shaking her head.

"Up through here." She motioned towards Michigan Avenue and up at the capitol. "The people who organized it asked everyone to stay in their vehicles because of the virus, but as you can see, no one is really listening. They're all heading up that way, so I hope you're not in a hurry."

"That doesn't make any sense," Mary commented, noting the abandoned vehicles. In the distance, as though to make her point, an ambulance was lying on the siren, but no one was there to clear their vehicles out of the way. The emergency vehicle, it appeared, had to take to the sidewalk in order to make any progress.

"Some of the other organizers are asking for people to tie up the area; bring traffic to a stop."

"Including blocking emergency vehicles?" Mary asked, the alarm clear in her voice.

The tired woman nodded, staring helplessly at the mass of parked cars and trucks. "They know we're here. Not sure what point they're trying to make, though."

"That's nuts?"

"Be safe." She stepped away, shaking her head in disgust.

"You too," Mary called out before the woman merged into the flow of human traffic migrating past the hospital's entrance.

Mary rolled up the window and looked over at her brother, who was staring at his phone. "Can you believe that?"

"You gotta do what you gotta do," he replied, never pulling his eyes from the tiny screen.

"Come again? You can't really be in favor of all this? These people are blocking emergency vehicles from reaching the E.R.? Their actions could literally end up costing someone their lives today!"

He looked up and studied his younger and only sister, her face flush. "Well, obviously not blocking traffic trying to get to the hospital."

"But you think the protestors here have a valid point? Thousands are dead or infected and we're being told to isolate and these folks are setting the objective back simply by showing up. Few of these people are wearing masks and some of them are carrying rifles!"

"You know, sis, it's legal to open-carry those," he replied, using the 'sis' in what she felt was always a patronizing way.

What pissed her off even more was their continued debate regarding the gun laws, but that was a separate issue that had, so far, not affected the virus grabbing hold of the planet. It would certainly gain publicity for the yahoos gathering here today, but they were going to cause the outbreak to get worse and prolong the agony for everyone. Block an ambulance and it could be traced directly to someone's death. Catch the virus and spread it? You would have no way of knowing how many people would end up dying from that careless act.

At events like today, where the huddled masses were congregating without even simple things like masks or staying spread out from one another, it wouldn't be the guns killing people, it would be these folks who would be the carriers spreading it to the far reaches of the state and beyond. To those smaller communities who were woefully unprepared to deal with such an outbreak.

The mask mandates, social distancing, and stay-at-home-orders were the extent of the tools that the government had at its disposal for nipping the outbreak in the bud. The government orders, that protests like this were actively trying to undo, would certainly succeed in more than offsetting the progress made by those following the laws and CDC guidelines.

She wanted to kick someone or something, but her brother was out of reach and she wasn't about to step out of the RV. So, like usual, with no immediate way of venting, she bottled up the fury and uncork it later.

The Winnebago continued to inch along, because those around them were also just passing through, or the protestors, fearing their vehicles wouldn't be here when they returned, reconsidered their options. In a few cases, Mary could see that hospital personnel, taking time away from their shifts, had stopped traffic with nothing more than their own bodies in order to clear paths for emergency traffic. Not everyone needing emergency care was suffering from a viral infection. People still suffered strokes or heart attacks and every second counted.

"God bless these folks," Mary muttered under her breath, as she pondered the hell that all these hospital workers were going through. And to continue their work despite being literally mocked by the individuals walking past the hospital as though they were at Mardi Gras. The crowds on the street were laughing and joking while their neighbors were a few floors up, in isolation, taking their final breaths. What the hell was the matter with these people? Mary wanted to scream at the top of her lungs.

She felt tears forming in her eyes, but like before, she willed them away for another time.

Where was God during episodes like these, she wondered again for the hundredth time? If he was hard to find in 'normal' times, shouldn't he be more apparent now? Their mother had always told them we'll never be able to see the wisdom of God's plan, but no matter what happens, He'll always use what looks like bad things for good. Like then, she was having trouble seeing how the pandemic could ever be used for something good. Enough pundits, though, both religious and secular, had weighed in on that very topic. One question and a million different answers.

As the RV edged its way through the light, making a left turn at the end of Michigan Avenue, Mary looked out her window at the open area in front of the capital. There were, at most, a hundred people huddled far too close together, several folks lined up on the steps near a makeshift podium to await their turn for a sound bite and a chance to be on the evening news.

Mary had been to this very place less than a year ago, standing in that same spot, listening to speakers talk about various social issues. It seemed like a natural spot for dissent to be aired, but today it seemed far different, and she wasn't entirely sure why. The guns were intimidating certainly, the anger palpable. But the Nazi and confederate flags? What place did those have here?

It felt like a lifetime ago, when the simple act of gathering together was something we all took for granted. Maybe that was God's plan, she thought, trying to make sense of it all. Make us more appreciative? I'll have to ask Him when I see God someday. Hopefully, it won't be soon.

She turned back to ask her brother his thoughts, to see if she was so far off base with her thoughts, and found him staring straight ahead. He was apparently oblivious to everything going on around them as he steered the RV around another corner and came to a stop again.

"What do you think?" she prompted.

"About?" he replied, looking her way.

Mary nodded out the window to her right, the gathering still in view.

"Obviously, they're using those flags to make a statement about the governor," he began, "but it also paints them in a terrible light. I would never feel right carrying those flags, but good for them for protesting their discontent."

Her brother held up a hand when she was about to protest his remarks, and then added, "But given that the virus is still spreading and Michigan is a hot-spot, they should be following the recommended guidelines."

The fire inside Mary dimmed somewhat at the asterisk he lofted onto the end of his comment, but she could feel it reignite when he continued his speech.

"I think she's gone too far, though," he said, referring to the current government mandates. "Some requirements are ridiculous. Many states aren't declaring shelter-in-place or even mask requirements. Those that have, and nearly a quarter of this state, including you and I, are unemployed," he said to make his point. "My job is probably going to be okay once the auto industry starts up again, but I worry about you and yours."

"'That woman from Michigan,'" as the president condescendingly referred to the governor, "has an impossible decision to make. They'll condemn her, no matter what happens."

Her brother nodded. "No doubt," he admitted. "That's why the president washed his hands of it all and threw the onus for the entire pandemic response, once it blew up in his face, back onto the states."

"The trouble stems from the fact that we'll never know how many lives were saved by the emergency declaration here in Michigan," Mary said.

"But we'll know if it goes south, sometimes literally, if more hotspots develop in places that aren't careful," he said, referring to places like Florida, Texas, and South Dakota. He leaned on the gas pedal as the bottleneck cleared.

Five minutes more and they finally reached their first planned destination. The brewery's front windows were dark though, and the Winnebago had the entire parking lot to itself. Mary knew from experience she could get passionate, but it was rare to see her brother lose his shit. Facing the locked door and the 'closed' sign, he was pacing erratically, arms flailing skyward.

"I cannot believe it's closed! Why is it closed?" he asked, in dramatic fashion. "Stupid emergency order!" James pressed his face up to the glass, eyes searching for any signs of life inside. God help any employee who got spotted by her brother, Mary prayed.

It was with a mix of pity and amusement that she let his ranting go on, unabated. The sign on the door of the brewery mentioned they had changed over their entire production to make much needed hand-sanitizer. Mary wished they were open so she could stock up on more of that anti-viral goop, because she suspected they could need it in the days to come. Might be handy to have an extra case or two with which to barter, she mused.

But her brother wasn't here for the sanitizer. He was here, she learned, for their special 'Joe in Black' Lager and right now, he was striking out.

He tried the doors again as if they had become magically unlocked, and made a noise of disgust she couldn't quite categorize when they hadn't.

"Come on, James, maybe they have it at a convenience store down the street," she consoled.

He eventually followed, taking one last look over his shoulder, but the lights remained off, nobody at home.

"Why would the convenience stores be open? I didn't know alcohol and Twinkies were essential!" he sneered, mocking the governor's order again.

This was going to be a long trip, Mary thought to herself as they climbed back into their seats and belted in.

"Listening to you going on and on, I'd have classified beer as essential," she added, half serious. "I could use one right about now."

They rolled towards the nearest store that Siri thought might be promising.

"They sell other things in these places, like milk and bread too, you know," Mary said, as they pulled into the parking lot and parked. But the few people coming out, she noted, weren't carrying any such practical items.

"At least you can still get your essential lottery tickets and scratch offs," he mocked.

Mary had to concede his point. If you could shop at a home-improvement store for essentials like appliances, but not buy paint or landscaping materials, she couldn't exactly defend lottery ticket sales if you popped in places like this for Diet Coke and Twinkies.

"All about the lottery sales," he mumbled as he climbed from the driver's seat. At least he was putting on his mask, as she watched him stomp towards the door. Before he could get inside, though, a gentleman stopped him in his tracks. She could see an exchange of words, but couldn't read their lips behind the masks. Her brother was waving his arms animatedly, pointing first towards the store, then pointing towards the RV, and finally towards what she assumed had to be the brewery a couple of blocks distant. The gentleman interacting with James appeared unswayed, though by any of her brother's passionate pleas.

"You shall not pass!" Mary boomed, her voice echoing in the camper as she quoted Gandalf's famous line from the Lord of the Rings. Then she started laughing to herself at the absurdity of their current situation. "This is just nuts."

A shopper stepped out of the convenience store, gave the two men a wide berth, and headed for her car. The gentleman turned, opened the door with his latex gloved hand, and waved her brother forward. There must have been too many people inside, Mary noted, when the gentleman stopped another approaching shopper in the same manner.

Wise to keep the number of bodies to a minimum, she thought, admiring the establishment for their reasonable application of the rules.

Minutes later, her brother emerged, a case of beer wrapped in his arms like he was protecting a newborn. She couldn't see his face under the mask, but Mary could imagine the smile, a fresh pep in his step betraying his joy. He climbed in back, returned his mask to his coat pocket, and stocked up the small fridge with a few beers. He passed her an Italian sub wrapped up tight in clear wrap, and tossed his on the driver's seat. Lunch would happen on the road, it seemed, as they tried to put some miles behind them before dark.

"I even bought my first lottery ticket just because I could!" he declared, slapping it for emphasis, as he climbed back behind the wheel, smiling, the frustration of the day already forgotten.

"And we're off!" he said with a flourish.

8 – South Bend, Indiana

They both climbed out of the Winnebago and stepped down to the cracked asphalt.

"There you go, sis. You can ask him all about His plan," James said, motioning towards a pair of individuals hanging out on the corner of the truck stop building.

Mary studied the two men as she and her brother approached the door. One who was wheelchair bound, while the second hovered over him. The seated man was waving his arms frantically, as the other man, standing almost on top of him now, was reaching forward as though trying to calm the man's crazy motion.

As they closed the distance, her brother corrected himself. "I was wrong. It actually looks like Zach

Galifianakis. The long hair and robe-like shirt threw me for a moment."

It finally dawned on Mary what her brother was insinuating, and she tossed him a dirty look. As the siblings neared the building and the unusual pair on the sidewalk under the awning, the man in the wheelchair, who had looked to be calming down, suddenly leaped unexpectedly to his feet and ran off around the side of the truck stop and out of view. It was so surprising that Mary and her brother both slowed their approach.

"Maybe you were right," Mary teased.

James looked unconvinced as he picked up speed again.

When 'Zach' spotted the siblings, he pushed off the curb and began walking quickly in their direction. Mary noted that James, sensing the man might have been angling to cut them the pair off, had picked up his pace and reached the door first, turning and smiling like he had just broken the tape on a hundred-meter dash. When James looked back, however, he was dismayed to find that Mary had slowed down, and Zach had taken a position between her and the door.

"I'll meet you inside," she called out.

Her brother looked skeptical, but eventually nodded, disappearing inside.

She looked down into the man's smiling face and introduced herself. "I'm Mary," she said, catching herself as she extended a hand in greeting. If it offended him when she pulled it back, he didn't show it.

"I'm Jesus," he replied, pronouncing it Hay-Zeus.

She smiled, wondering how he could have heard them from clear across the parking lot, but soon realized that neither she nor James had used the name Jesus in their comments as they had approached the truck-stop on foot.

"Did you know that my mother's name was Mary?" he asked.

She nodded in acknowledgement, unphased by the coincidence.

"I really miss her cooking," he added.

The man who had been wheelchair bound only moments earlier came back into view, glared at the pair, then shook his head before disappearing again.

"What was the problem with him?" she asked.

"He's got some really wicked demons in him," Jesus replied. "Well, he *did* have really wicked demons, past tense, in him, technically." They watched for a few more moments, but the man didn't reappear.

"And the walking part?" Mary asked, the wheelchair now abandoned.

Jesus waved his hands nonchalantly. "Ahh, that's nothing."

"It didn't look like nothing to me," she replied honestly. "Even more so to him, I bet."

He appraised her for a moment and, noting the sincerity, seemed almost embarrassed by the kind words. "That's very nice of you to say. Thank you."

Mary, picturing her brother's growing impatience at her absence, turned towards the door. "I know it won't measure up to mom's home cooking, but would you like to join us for dinner?" she asked, motioning towards the door. "My treat."

"Really? I'd love to. Thank you."

Both freshened upped before climbing into the booth opposite her brother, who hadn't bothered to look up from his phone as they sat down. Mary passed a menu to Jesus and then scoured the hundred plus offerings on her own copy for something appealing to eat.

When her brother looked up, he paused, froze, eyes widening ever so slightly. Mary had been watching him, waiting for a reaction, and when it came, she had to fight off the urge not to laugh at the absurdity of the situation. His eyes slid from their guest over to his sister, back and forth again. She could see the gears in his head turn, trying to make sense of what was happening. He was used to his sister's spontaneity over the years and had gotten better at his reactions, she happily noted. James stifled a comment, sagging only slightly in a sign of practiced resignation.

"Jesus has decided to join us for dinner," she declared. Although she was reading through the menu, Mary could still see her brother's face in her periphery. He was looking at their dining companion, but trying not to stare. She felt his gaze swing back in her direction, but she wouldn't give in and look up at him. After a few moments, Mary watched as James turned his attention back to the menu, choosing to remain silent.

"Everyone decide?" the server asked. The woman looked like she had worked here for decades and wasn't the type to be trifled with.

Mary always made sure she had a go-to meal right away for just such circumstances, but used the remaining time to peruse for something more appealing. People say you can't live on burgers alone, but she didn't think that was the case. "Burger, medium, with American cheese, hold the tomato. Fries, coleslaw and a Diet Pepsi, please," Mary said, carefully noting that only Pepsi products were available at this establishment.

The server, without looking up, seemed pleased by Mary's preparation.

Her brother weighed in with several questions on a couple of entrees, and her patience seemed to have evaporated. If James had noticed, and Mary rarely detected that he did, it didn't show. She suspected her brother didn't do it on purpose, but he was just very particular about what he put in his body. Unfortunately, this wasn't the type of place he frequented. The server looked at Mary for help.

'Sorry,' she mouthed. The server guessed correctly and just nodded, assuming that Mary had had to put up with this sort of thing for years.

"I'll go with the hummus platter," he started, then clarified. "Are the stuffed grape leaves vegetarian, vegan, and or gluten-free?"

She stared at him for a moment, but didn't answer.

James nodded, waving her off. "It sounds good. I'll go with it, anyway."

"Drink?" she asked.

"Do you have bottled water?"

The server paused again, wondering if he was the one who was paying or not and if it was worth risking a measly tip.

"Filtered, but it's good. And before you ask, our ice is made from the same filtered water."

He nodded, confirming her assessment.

"And for you?" she asked, turning to Jesus.

"Also going Greek this evening with the gyro platter, fries and pita bread, please. Also, a Diet Pepsi."

The woman nodded her approval and moved down the rows of booths, checking on her other customers.

"Jesus, this is my brother, James. James," she said, motioning unnecessarily to their guest. "This is Jesus."

"Pleasure," James said, the smallest hint of a smirk on her brother's lips, a twinkle in his eyes as he shot a look towards Mary.

"Likewise," Jesus replied, apparently unaware of the inside joke her brother had made about him in the parking lot earlier.

The food arrived, and the plates were laid out. Mary bowed her head, about to say Grace, catching her brother in mid-bite. He didn't regularly give thanks these days, but out of respect, he laid his fork down and bowed his head.

"Heavenly Father," Mary began, but then paused, unmoving, a stray thought striking her. If this was truly *the* Jesus, what would the protocol be exactly in a situation like this?

She noticed James open one eye and look up at her, head still bowed, wondering about the delay, so she finished. "We'd like to thank you for this food we are about to enjoy, the spiritual guidance and love you always provide, and for all the blessings you continue to provide in our lives. Amen."

"Amen. Very nice," Jesus commented, smiling at her while squeezing ketchup on his fries.

Mary felt herself blush slightly, pleased by the appraisal. When she looked up, her brother was staring at her, with a peculiar grin on his face while he slathered pita bread with garlic sauce. She tossed him an annoyed look and then turned her attention to her own meal.

"How the gyro?" she inquired.

"Delicious," he replied, dumping more tzatziki on the dish.

"I assumed you didn't eat lamb?" her brother asked.

Mary was as much surprised by the question as by James feeling compelled to converse with their dining companion. In similar settings with strangers, she often had to prod him along just to be social.

Seemingly unfazed by the inquiry, Jesus took another hearty bite. "Oh, no, lamb has always been one of my favorites."

"Good to know," James said, before retreating into his own thoughts.

They ate in silence for a few minutes before Jesus spoke again. "There are few things in life as intimate as a meal shared with friends."

James had stopped mid-bite because he didn't know how to respond, Mary suspected. For her, though, it was different. She had paused because of the sentiment that the statement carried. The poetic beauty of its simplicity and wisdom had struck her solidly, and with a weight she hadn't expected.

She looked around the truck stop, which had a worn and tired industrial look. Most people sitting in this place were heading somewhere and had simply stopped to eat. No one else, she imagined, dining with others here, or anywhere frankly, would think of their meals as an intimate experience. She and James certainly weren't thinking about it, ever, until Jesus just casually tossed it out there and took another bite.

Would she ever think about eating the same way again? The world can be a distracting place, but she felt a need to hold on to this bit of wisdom and file it away for safekeeping. It would help her appreciate the small things she never gave a second thought to.

Mary wanted to ask more questions, but none of them seemed worthy.

"Live in the area, Jesus?" her brother asked, unknowingly letting Mary off the hook.

"No. Just passing through, like you," he said.

"Where do you call home?" James continued, clearly curious, but she didn't know what he might be getting at.

"Born in Bethlehem, but I grew up around Nazareth." he replied, wiping up the last of his ketchup with the final fry.

James exchanged a look with Mary, a playful smirk on his lips, before she asked for them both. "Israel?"

"Pennsylvania," Jesus answered.

"Of course." James chuckled, pushing his plate away.

"Well, I hate to eat and run, but I really need to be going," Jesus said, getting to his feet suddenly and bowing slightly. "Thank you for my meal and for the wonderful company."

Mary was bummed that they were parting company so quickly, but knew that he was saving them all from an awkward goodbye.

"Please, don't get up on my account. Thank you again," he continued, before stepping away.

"It was nice to meet you," she replied, waving.

They finished a few more bites before deciding it was time to get back on the road themselves.

"We need to get going too," her brother commented, as it got dark outside.

9 – Bolingbrook, Illinois

Mary awoke with a start, not recognizing her surroundings. She tried to think back to where she might be, but it was the familiar smell of the Winnebago that brought a flood of emotions washing over her. And grief, realizing everything she had lost recently; her father, her job, her mission, her motivation. It all felt overwhelming until thoughts of Jesus came to mind and the distraction proved medicinal.

She heard the door to the RV open and seconds later felt the entire vehicle rock. "I hope that's you."

"Nope," came the familiar voice.

Despite the grogginess, her nose picked up on a fresh scent, stomach growling. "You got donuts and tea?" she asked, as she whipped the curtain aside and stepped out.

"You're half right," he said, sipping on what she had to assume was his first beer of the day.

Her brother winced, watching as she poured out the drink from the cardboard carafe and slugged down the piping hot liquid as though it were only lukewarm. "I can't believe you're drinking that. Felt like I was burning my hand, just carrying it over here."

She simply sighed, soaking up the goodness. It hadn't been a great night for her. The campground where they had been planning to stop for the night was closed because of the state of emergency. The presumptions they had made in their lives, PV (pre-virus), no longer seemed to apply. Assumptions that were later proven to be true, were in the minority these days. Having the RV now seemed like a genius move, and Mary had to give her brother credit.

She sat down and dug into the bag, looking for something fried, and either frosting covered or custard filled. Neither were present.

"They don't have donuts there," he said, noting her disappointment. "Lucky to get those. The counter is closed up tight and only the drive through is open. I offered somebody coming through the line to order for us, since you can't do it on foot it seems and the Winnebago is over the height limit, but they wouldn't take my money."

She smiled inwardly, finding the stranger's reluctance to benefit from the situation to be a grand gesture, although her skeptic nature had initially assumed the worst. It was something she had struggled with for years and knew it was something she really needed to work on. Were there bad people in this world looking to take advantage of such situations? Sure, and there always would be. But she also knew that there were good folks to be found if you went looking for them.

"I wonder where he is at this moment?" Mary mused.

James' eyes narrowed, head turning towards her in confusion.

"Jesus," she clarified. "I wonder where he went after we left."

James shrugged in that indifferent way that Mary had always known. He clearly hadn't given the mysterious stranger, with whom they had eaten dinner only last night, a second thought.

"Don't know. Why?"

Mary knew there was really no reason that she could put her finger on. She had been running the events of last evening over and over in her mind, wondering if she could ever end up in similar circumstances. Without her brother in her life, she could easily lose her job, if she even still had one, she realized, and with no close relatives to help her, nor any real close friends who could provide help, she too could quickly find herself on the streets.

She had friends, but when push came to shove, could she count on any of them for more than a few days of help?

Without such social safety nets, Mary knew she was only a couple of weeks away from being in the same precarious position as Jesus, assuming he was indeed a man down on his luck and not just someone who lived such a lifestyle by choice.

"What if he really was, you know?" She asked, words trailing off.

With the tipped-up bottle to his lips, James paused, eyes turning down towards Mary.

"God?" he clarified.

Mary thought it funny that James could so easily utter the word, but she hesitated. "Yes."

"You don't honestly believe that, do you?"

She laughed, rummaging through the treat bag, trying to stall.

"No, I guess not."

"You guess not?" James asked, sitting down across from her.

"No, he clearly isn't God," Mary replied, but it felt wrong to voice the opinion out loud. "This is just a hypothetical exercise. Seemed relevant given we just lost dad." Death had a way of bringing on such introspective examinations, she knew, from when they had lost their mother.

James nodded, looking relieved.

"Would be cool though, wouldn't it?" she asked, saying it with a bit more gusto in case God had truly been listening in on their conversation.

Her brother moved to speak, mouth opening, but nothing came out at first.

"I suppose so," he finally admitted, though it didn't seem enthusiastic. He finished his one and only beer and tucked it back into the case under the sink.

"Are we out of here?" she asked, giving up on the line of inquiry. "Want me to drive?"

Her brother slipped on his mask and shook his head.

"I'm going to run into Costco and grab some supplies. Want anything specific? Besides donuts," he asked, before she could swallow her mouthful of egg-white souffle.

That was very thoughtful of him, Mary thought to herself, noting that James seemed to step up to make this trip a success. They hadn't always gotten along so well, but they only had each other now, and maybe that made the difference.

"No, I'm good with whatever you're getting."

Mary grabbed another souffle and then followed in her brother's wake. It was brisk outside, but with the hoodie on and piping hot tea in hand, the cool morning air actually felt invigorating, rather than biting. She watched as James strolled across the parking lot, headed for the big box store, feeling guilty for not going with him. Mary got over it quickly when she saw the entrance line snaking along the front of the building. She was pleased to see at least a few feet between the customers.

Why weren't there more crimes being committed by masked people these days? Wouldn't the pandemic make it perfect cover? When else would you be able to walk around with a mask on and not look suspicious?

"Where in the world do these thoughts come from, Mary?" she asked herself, questioning her sanity yet again. And chastising herself for the inherent cynicism even though it was just a hypothetical exercise.

A form appeared on her right side, keeping the required distance, but its sudden, unexpected appearance made her jump, the last mouthful of breakfast stifling her yelp.

Jesus was also studying the building and shoppers, noting the line outside. "It's been kind of messy there in year's past, especially during the Black Friday sales, but they seem really well behaved this morning. That makes me happy."

Mary looked around, wondering where he could have come from, but there weren't many vehicles parked this far out in the lot near their RV. Washing down the last bite of her breakfast and feeling her pulse returning to normal, she finally felt capable of speaking. "Good morning."

"And a very blessed morning to you," Jesus said, turning and smiling in her direction. "It's really something, isn't it?" he asked, eyes on the skies.

"Sure is," she replied, not immediately seeing what he was referring to.

"The morning," Jesus clarified, noting her confusion.

"Oh, yes, it's lovely."

Was he following us?

"Do you have any more tea?" he inquired.

"Oh, I'm sorry. How rude of me. Yes, please, we have plenty inside and I can make more if we need it."

It surprised Mary how easily she had just invited a practical stranger into their RV, without so much as a second thought. "Please, help yourself," she offered, pointing at the bench seat and brown paper sack.

"I love their chocolate pastries," he said, selecting one.

Mary handed him one of the aged turquoise plastic mugs from the RV's retro collection, topped it off with tea from the carafe, and then sat down next to him. "We don't have any milk or sugar yet," she apologized. "I can call James to make sure he grabs some," she said, reaching for her cell phone.

"This is great, as-is, thank you."

A few seconds passed before Jesus spoke again.

"Is that your dad?" he asked, nodding towards the far end of the bench seat.

Without looking back, her eyes widened a little, picturing the stained wooden box still securely belted in the seat behind her. She nodded, wondering whether having him out in the open, his favorite baseball cap still in place, might have been over the top, despite how appropriate it had felt.

"The hat is a nice touch," he added, as though reading her thoughts. "He would have loved it. And he's very proud of you and your brother."

She smiled, feeling a lump building in her throat as raw emotions bottled up insider her once again threatened to come unwound. Jesus offered her a napkin from the bag just as a lone tear overflowed onto Mary's cheek. She gratefully wiped it away.

"Thank you," she whispered. She wasn't one who found it easy to speak about herself to many people, James included, but Jesus was different, she realized. When he looked at her, she got the impression than nothing and no one else mattered. Jesus lived in that moment with her, and gave his undivided attention, a skill sorely lacking in today's world.

Questions, followed by answers, flowed back and forth, but Jesus proved a better listener. The discussion eventually turned to Mary, her loss, the turmoil in her life, and her aspirations. Minutes turned into nearly an hour before the door to the RV opened and James climbed inside.

"We're going with plan 'B'," he declared, pausing when he found the two of them seated at the hideaway table.

"Which is?" Mary inquired.

"We head down the road and stop at the first store that doesn't have a line. Could I talk to you for a moment?" he asked, motioning for his sister to follow him outside.

"There's more tea if you want a refill," she said to Jesus, before exiting and closing the door behind them.

"Where did he come from?"

She shook her head and shrugged. "Not sure. It's like he just materialized out of thin air."

"Is he following us?"

"No. At least I don't think so. Maybe. Maybe not. Doesn't matter."

"How much tea have you had?"

"Not a lot. Why?" Mary replied, unsure what he was getting at.

"Are we ready, then?"

Mary nodded, but she looked sheepish. "I know I should have asked you first, but I told Jesus we'd give him a lift."

"What? We don't even know him. Don't you know you're not supposed to pick up hitch hikers, Mary?"

"Is he technically a hitch hiker though?"

"Seriously, we're going to get into semantics here? We only met him yesterday and then magically run into him again today? He doesn't have a vehicle of his own and you're offering rides. I think by most people's definition that makes him a hitch hiker!"

"I know," she defended, hands up. "But I feel like I know him. Is that weird?"

"Mary, I didn't think you did drugs, but you're acting way out there today."

"I'm not on drugs, James," she defended, but the words trailed off as the reminder of their loss crept back into her head. Mary wasn't so sure this trip was really such a great idea, given that their father had died only a few days ago. No reason that his ashes couldn't wait a few months or years to be spread. Why did she feel compelled it had to be done so soon?

"And we're not even sure exactly where we're going. Where is he going?"

"West," she admitted. "Nowhere specific, just west."

James exhaled loudly; adrenaline chasing away the chill in the air.

"Okay. West it is. Can we go now, before I change my mind?"

She nodded, relieved that her brother had agreed to her imposing request.

James returned to the driver's seat, not fully trusting his sister to drive, given her bizarre state. Mary seemed content to ride shotgun, strapping in next to him. She turned and smiled back at Jesus, trying to make it look sincere, but doubt was gnawing at her from the inside. Jesus was sitting there quietly nursing his second cup of tea, a pleasurable look beaming back at her.

"Thank you for giving me a lift," he said. "It's very gracious of you."

Unsure of what to say, James reached back and flashed a big thumbs up before dropping the RV in gear and pointing it westward, destination unknown.

10 – Aurora, Illinois

Fifteen minutes up the road, a small, family-style grocery store with only a few folks queued up outside came into view. James swung the RV in and all three of them masked up and wandered towards the door. An occasional shopper would emerge pushing a full cart and the person at the front of the line would slip inside.

Despite the short line, James was shifting impatiently from one foot to the other. Mary seemed indifferent to the delay, choosing instead to enjoy the warmth of the sunlight cascading down upon her. It was still chilly, Mary would admit, but she felt a lightness in her bones and a sense of purpose in her soul. She looked around and found that Jesus, while still keeping his social distance to the recommended

CDC guidelines, was working his way along the queue of people behind them, chatting with those who had fallen in at the end of the line.

The closer they got to getting in, the more impatient her brother was becoming, Mary noted. "We're almost there, James," she said, trying to soothe him.

"This wouldn't be happening in Japan." he said, turning towards her.

"No?" she asked, wondering where in the world this line of logic was leading.

"The Japanese government is proposing that only the men, in family households, should be allowed to do the shopping because female shoppers take too long."

"Is that right?" Mary had read the recent headlines and the same reports. She didn't have a poker-face, but the mask she was wearing made it that much easier to yank her brother's chain without him realizing it.

"Won't ever happen," she continued with confidence. "Though I'd love to see that."

Knowing how misogynistic the east-Asian society could be, and that shopping was a task that was solidly associated with women, it would never be more than a novelty recommendation.

"Why is that?" her brother asked.

"The society is far too gender-centric. Men there would never go for it. They'd rather starve, I imagine."

"Think they've started helping with the housework or childcare while sheltering at home?" he asked.

"No," she said quickly, having given this story and its ramifications plenty of thought over the past few weeks. She was also surprised that James hadn't presented the question sarcastically. Maybe he was growing inside and truly pondering the changes that the pandemic was causing to the traditional roles and relationships in every society affected by the virus.

"Why is that? Think men are lazy?" her brother asked, making sure he was facing Mary when he did so. Even with the mask in place, Mary could see that he was grinning. He loved trying to catch her in illogical arguments, particularly if they were hypothetical.

"No, men are often far less discerning in the cleanliness of their habitats when they're the ones charged with doing the cleaning."

He could picture his own place back in Michigan. "Point taken," James conceded without debate.

A young couple, with two very young children in their cart, rolled out of the store without masks on. Mary shook her head and mumbled under her own mask, trying to give the inconsiderate parents the stink eye, but neither seemed to notice her passive-aggressive protest.

"Don't worry. All of them will be fine," Jesus said, answering their unasked question as he reappeared suddenly by their side.

Mary and James exchanged glances, neither knowing exactly how to respond.

Before an awkward silence ensued, the gatekeeper controlling traffic at the door waved at the three of them and they could proceed.

The store itself wasn't huge, so the variety normally found on the shelves wasn't large. There were only one or two options to choose from for each product type, so it was easy to decide. It was clear, though, that despite the employees working quickly, there were gaps in what was available. Mary and her brother, sharing a cart, stayed together and, with the options being slim to none, were able to quickly find and grab what they needed.

"Where did all the toilet paper go?" Mary asked, noting the empty gap in the shelves. James' mind, however, wasn't on the missing paper products.

"You just heard him!" James whispered under his breath, after Jesus had split off from the pair, heading towards the meat counter along the back wall of the store.

"I heard him say that they'll be fine," Mary replied, distracted. Her eyes watched as a cart swung past, heaped high with TP, paper towel, and boxes of tissues. Other shoppers had done the same, explaining away the mystery that had confounded her moments ago but not explaining why people felt the need to horde such things. Mary was going to inquire with the next paper product poacher she came across, but James seemed insistent on having her full, undivided attention.

"And you don't see anything wrong with his fortune-telling?" he asked, tugging at her jacket sleeve.

"We don't know what he meant. Maybe it was in a general sort of way. Wishful thinking," she replied, turning towards him.

"Don't know what he meant?" James asked incredulously. "How else could you have interpreted his comment? He's implying that they'll not be affected by the virus. That he knows it for a fact!"

She gave up on finding any avocados that weren't already past their prime and moved on to the strawberries. "With only a three percent fatality rate being reported, and despite their casualness in being out in public, chances are they *will* be fine, statistically speaking."

James eyed Mary skeptically, unable to tell for sure if she was trying to use his own argument against him or not, the damn mask hiding most of her telling features.

"We should go," he said flatly, looking around and not spying Jesus anywhere.

Mary nodded and motioned towards the checkout line, missing his intentions.

"I mean, without you know who," he added, trying to beat another cart to the cashier.

"Jesus? You just want to leave without him?"

"He might be dangerous," James offered.

"He's not dangerous," Mary defended, without evidence.

"You have no way of knowing that! He could have escaped from someplace."

Mary stared at her brother with a mix of curiosity and frustration, wondering where all this sudden angst was coming from. She was going to respond, but the flow of her brother's arguments just kept spilling out.

"Look, I'm sure he can easily find another ride. This place is on a busy roadway and there's a bunch of traffic. He got this far, didn't he? Covered the same distance we did, all without a vehicle. And he could get a ride with a trucker and cover far more miles than he ever could hope to with us and the Winnebago."

James edged the cart further forward, garnering backward stares from the shopper on which he was clearly encroaching.

"No," Mary replied flatly, arms crossed. "We're not just abandoning him here. You can't abandon someone once you've promised to take them somewhere."

James stared up at the ceiling, trying to calm himself.

"We did promise," Mary reminded him, but James was ready for it.

"To take him west and technically, we did that!"

"Only ten miles."

"But it was technically west," he defended, finger raised in a 'gotcha' sort of way. "How far 'west' are we contractually obligated to take him exactly?"

"Over ten miles," was all Mary added.

"Are you sure you haven't taken any drugs? I'm not going to judge you if you did." James queried, revisiting the topic again while quickly unloading their few items onto the short belt.

The woman at the register paused for only a moment, her eyes meeting Mary's.

"I'm not and I don't," she answered both the woman and her brother at once.

"But if you were?"

"Yes, James, I would tell you," she said, hoping this was the end of his inquiry.

Even the credit card processing seemed to take its sweet time today, as James impatiently waited for the approval. Mary noted that if he had paid cash, they would already be halfway across the parking and nearing the RV.

She looked back for Jesus, but didn't see him. If the time came and she refused to get back into the Winnebago, would James pull away without her? He might justify leaving Jesus behind, but surely, he wouldn't get back on the road with her standing in the parking lot, would he?

James was reaching for his wallet, ready to grab some cash instead when, to Mary's delight and James' dismay, Jesus had miraculously appeared once again at their side.

Mary heard her brother mumble something under his breath, just as the credit slip printer dispensed his receipt, but failed to catch the words.

"Are you alright?" Mary asked, noticing a change in her new friend.

Jesus nodded, coat bundled up, arms crossed. "Cold in here."

"Are you sure? You look uncomfortable," she asked with genuine concern.

He nodded. "Fine."

Both James and the woman behind the hastily installed plexiglass divider eyed the man suspiciously, then looked at one another. James shrugged and wheeled the cart for the exit.

Setting the bags in the back of the Winnebago, they were on the road again in seconds. With her brother behind the wheel, Mary thought she would take the time to store their meager purchases. When she climbed over the center console and slid in back, she paused at the unexpected scene laid out on the table in front of her.

"I thought we might fire up the grill for lunch and enjoy this bounty," Jesus offered, working a filet knife with what appeared to be practiced skill. Maybe he used to work in a kitchen, she thought to herself, knowing that so many restaurants in the world had been quickly shuttered, their employees laid off during the pandemic.

Her brother, normally prone to skepticism and cynicism, had grown quiet up front, undoubtedly perturbed that his attempt to ditch their guest had been foiled. Knowing that Jesus was back here wielding such a nasty-looking knife wouldn't have helped James' disposition any, she so kept it to herself.

"Where did that come from?" Mary asked, while she emptied the grocery bags and stored the contents.

"What?" he asked.

"The fish," she said, motioning to the large salmon stretched across the table between them.

"Are we talking philosophically? Biologically?"

"Metaphysically?" she said with a smile.

Jesus spread with his arms out wide to the side, his chest pumped up, like the answer should have been obvious.

"Didn't I feed over five thousand with just a few fish and some loaves?"

Mary knew that the real Jesus had done that, as recorded in the gospels, but wasn't sure it was necessarily healthy for the Jesus sitting in front of her to think that he had. Mary didn't need to turn, feeling her brother's eyes on them via the rearview mirror. Apparently, he was paying close attention to their conversation, and she didn't need to ask James to know what he was thinking at this point.

"Didn't you, like, have to start with some fish and multiply them? 0 times infinity still equals zero, doesn't it?" she challenged, deciding it was harmless at this stage to play along.

Jesus looked at her confused. "You mean like dough loaded with yeast?"

"Well, I guess so. I know we don't have any fish in the fridge or freezer."

"I created the entire universe out of nothing, remember?" he waved his hands over the prepped fish with a flourish. "But you think this would be impossible?"

He made that move again with his arms like she had seen David Copperfield do in Vegas a few years back. Maybe Jesus was an out of work magician?

"Valid point," she conceded with a laugh.

Jesus seemed pleased, as he finished up and laid the skillfully prepared filets on a plate that Mary had provided.

"But if you must know, I started with those," he offered, pointing towards the narrow cupboard to her left.

"These?" she asked, holding up the bag of goldfish crackers.

"Those are both fish *and* loaves."

"But they're not even opened," she commented, tipping it to prove her point.

"Seriously?" he asked, implying that the answer should now be perfectly obvious. "The universe from nothing, and a closed bag could stop me?"

"That seems sketchy," she replied, trying to sound dubious but failing.

"Oh look," Jesus exclaimed, opening the fish's mouth and retrieving something from inside. He held out a fist towards Mary, questioning her with a stare that asked if she trusted him.

Mary stared at the hand for a moment, unsure. She eyed him with a raised eyebrow, wondering if she dared hold out her hand to receive whatever he had found inside the salmon. Even when the worst-case scenario didn't look all that bad, Mary still hesitated, as though this simple act was far bigger than having something gross dumped in her palm.

"Consider it a test of faith," he said, motioning again with his fist.

Reluctantly, she reached out but didn't open her hand.

"I can't put something new and exciting in there, unless you're open to receive it, Mary," he continued, watching her with an intensity she had never seen before. He nodded when she was on the verge of reaching a favorable conclusion.

Her fist unwound slowly but was fully prepared to drop the item like it was hot, should it be something slimy or disgusting.

But she needn't worry. The tumbling object flashed in the daylight as it fell through the air. When it landed flat on her palm, she immediately recognized it as a gold-colored Sacagawea, US, one-dollar coin. Her gaze studied the tiny treasure.

"I haven't seen one of these in a while, even though hundreds of millions were minted," she said, trying to hand it back.

"Oh no, it's not mine," he replied, refusing it.

"It belongs to the fish?"

Jesus shrugged. "I guess so. Don't think he'll be needing it, though."

"What is that smell?" James asked, finally speaking up. "That isn't fish, is it? Where did we get fish?"

Mary and Jesus were both laughing now.

"It's a long story," Mary replied, turning towards Jesus in a conspiratorial way.

"He hates fish," she whispered, shaking her head.

"He hasn't tried mine," Jesus winked.

"And I don't think that's enough to feed five-thousand people though," she challenged Jesus.

"Are we expecting company?" he asked.

11 – Shabbona, Illinois

Surprised to find the state park open, they paid their admission and drove until they located a secluded spot with a view of the lake. The gas grill fired up quickly as they prepared to have lunch and take a break. Intent on carrying his weight, Jesus shooed the siblings to the picnic table nearby while he slathered the salmon in various spices and covered each in lemon slices before wrapping the filets in foil and setting them onto the hot grate.

It didn't take long for the smells to wash over the pair, James still looking dubious.

"Did we pick up hotdogs earlier?" he asked, looking pouty.

"Keep an open mind," Mara chastised, pushing the Doritos bag his way.

"You're the adventurous one with trying new restaurants and foods," he said, not meaning it as the compliment it appeared, but Mary smiled proudly. She liked to think she was open to new experiences. And she hoped the salmon was as good as it smelled because her stomach was rumbling and the chips were no longer cutting it.

"Here we go!" Jesus said, setting a heavy foil pouch in front of each of them.

"Tartar sauce?" James asked hopefully.

Jesus looked indignant at the very suggestion.

Mary elbowed her brother. "Sorry. We didn't know we were being treated to this delicious fish."

They bowed their heads and Mary said grace, not experiencing the sense of doubt that had come upon her during their first meal together.

It didn't have the typical smell to it, James noted with relief, as he pulled open the pouch, a hint of lemon vapor drifting skyward.

"Where did we get lemons?" he asked her.

Mary looked at Jesus, who simply threw his arms wide, smiling.

James timidly forked in a mouthful, cautious. That he hadn't immediately reached for his beer was a promising sign, she noted.

"Not bad," he finally declared.

Mary had to agree. It was marvelous. "So good."

Jesus, not looking surprised by their assessment, beamed as he dug into his own portion.

"Did your mother teach you to cook like this?" Mary asked, remembering their earlier conversation.

Jesus laughed heartily, nearly choking, apparently some kind of inside joke only he was privy to.

"It certainly wasn't my earthly father. He could work wood like no one else, but for meal preparation, mom learned long ago not to get him involved. He either burned everything or it fell into the fire."

Mary sensed a lull there as Jesus grew quiet. Maybe it was memories coming back. She knew she was in the same boat as he, both parents nothing more than memories.

"Are you named after my mother?" Jesus asked unexpectedly.

"I am," Mary replied, continuing to play along.

He nodded. "Nice."

"And I'm named after your brother," James added, as he stepped away to pack up the grill.

After her brother had moved beyond hearing them speak, Mary looked at Jesus and shook her head.

"Dad loved Gene Wilder, and his favorite movie, Blazing Saddles, had just come out," Mary said.

"I love that movie! One of my all-time favorites."

"Really?" she asked, surprised. Would the Son of God even have a favorite movie, she wondered?

12 – Rockford, Illinois

"Oh my God!" James exclaimed from the driver's seat as he slowed the Winnebago down again.

"Yes, my son?" Jesus mumbled incoherently from the back, still dozing.

"Another toll booth. I can't believe it." James shook his head in disgust.

Mary rooted around in her purse, not finding the change to get them through and it was an unmanned booth.

"Not enough?" her brother asked, too far in to move over, with traffic already closing in from behind. "The locals in this state must drive around with a bag of coins at the ready."

"Wait!" she said, patting down the pockets of her jeans. Triumphantly, Mary withdrew the last coin in the RV, the exact amount needed. She handed it to her brother, who eyed it with suspicion.

"Not sure the machine will take it," he said, leaning out the window.

"It's legal currency. I think it has to work."

James dropped the coins in the chute and after a few seconds of suspense, the toll gate climbed obediently out of the way and their path ahead was clear.

When Jesus eventually awoke, the RV was still rolling along. But Mary, who had been riding shotgun earlier, was now seated at the other end of the bench seat, eating goldfish crackers, her gaze silently assessing him. She tipped the small bag in his direction, offering a share.

"Thank you."

He sat up straighter and stretched, looking outside while Mary continued to stare as though focusing her attention would provide an obvious answer to the crazy question that continued to nag at her. None appeared though, so she tried the old-fashioned approach.

"Are you really Him?" she asked.

"It's really about whether you believe."

She leaned in closer to get a better look at him, as though there might be some kind of maker's mark on his forehead. When Mary didn't respond, Jesus continued.

"It didn't work out so well for me the last time I answered that question truthfully," he conceded, a pained look momentarily passing over his face.

"Too soon?" she asked, regretting their conversation had turned heavy, but she felt compelled to push.

"Kind of hard to forget," he admitted, rubbing his hands and wrists.

13 - Lena, Illinois

They reached the campground they were aiming for, but weren't overly excited to see it deserted, save for a sedan parked out front. When they pulled in, an older gentleman was just stepping out of the office, locking up.

"Not open?" Mary inquired, as she climbed from the Winnebago.

"Sorry, not yet. Normally would be, but," his voice fading away, a shrug of his shoulders. The rain had stopped, but a breeze was picking up, the man pulling his coat closer around him. "If you were to come back in an hour and park over there," he said, nodding with his chin off to one side, "and were gone by ten a.m. tomorrow, I wouldn't know anything about it. No fires though, please. Somebody would probably report that."

He smiled and waved as he lowered his tired frame into the driver's seat.

"Thank you," James called out through the passenger window, switching the RV into reverse. Mary nodded and waved.

"Let's grab dinner and figure out what we're going to do about tonight," he said, the unanswered question left hanging.

They could have eaten any number of things that they had in the RV, but since it wasn't wise to fire up the grill, they opted for the only place in the area that looked like it was open.

The parking lot wasn't too busy, so they could get inside and be seated with the required spacing. Probably not legally required in the state, but Mary was happy to see that the hostess had left a gap of a single booth between them and the next closest diners. They were handed freshly cleaned menus, the scent of strong bleach still lingering. It was riskier than disposable, she noted, but it was still kudos in her book.

No one else in the room was wearing masks, but they each had food in front of them, so it was only logical.

"I can't wait to see how they're going to eat with those things on," she heard the woman from the nearest booth say to the server.

Mary leaned over to one side and looked around her brother's head, eyes spying the woman in question. She was facing Mary's direction, while an older gentleman she presumed to be the woman's husband was seated in their booth with his back to them. He either hadn't responded, or Mary hadn't heard it. The server, a young woman, nodded in that practiced way which conveyed to the customer that they agreed with them, without really committing to it. She cleared a few plates before stepping over to the trio's booth, ready to take their order.

"What are you having tonight?" the woman asked, noticing that they all appeared ready to order.

"Are your salad ingredients all organic?" James inquired.

Mary didn't need to look over at the neighboring booth, as the woman, who had been going on and on at a high volume, fell silent. Jesus didn't seem to react, his eyes still perusing the specials that were paper clipped to the front of his menu.

"Fresh, yes. I seriously doubt they're organic," she said, doing her best to keep her face passive.

"Let's just go with the salad then," James said.

"Dressing?"

"Do you have poppy seed?"

The server first squinted at James, trying to detect any sign that the man was trying to be difficult, then looked over at Mary, who wore a sheepish 'sorry' look on her face, lips pursed.

"Ranch. I'll take the ranch." he said, turning towards Mary. "Why do they always look at you when I'm ordering?"

For her part, she just shrugged.

"For you?"

"Cheeseburger, medium, with the fries and coleslaw, Diet Pepsi."

"You got it, Hon," she said, making the mental note. "And finally, for you?" she asked Jesus.

"Is your salmon farmed or line caught?"

"Line caught," she answered.

"Sustainably?"

"Definitely."

"I'll have that. Baked potato, butter, sour cream, but no bacon," Jesus finished.

"Why do they always look at *me* funny when I ask questions?" her brother mumbled under his breath, clearly unhappy about being on the wrong end of the double standard.

"It's weird," she said, dodging the question. Mary clearly did not want to open that can of worms before the server had even stepped away from the booth.

With that task completed and a few minutes to wait for their food, Mary slipped back into listening in on their nearest neighbors.

"I don't know what the big fuss is about. People die from the flu every year!"

The man across from her grunted, not in a way that signified agreement, but an acknowledgement that he had heard her.

"The president says there's nothing to worry about. He wouldn't lie!"

Grunt.

Mary had only partially stifled her cough at that remark.

"It's these immigrants coming here for our jobs. They should be more grateful!"

Grunt.

Mary wasn't entirely sure what being grateful had to do with the issue.

"If they didn't live in packs, then the virus wouldn't be spreading all over. It's not their workplace causing it!"

Grunt.

"Besides, that 'China virus' is all their doing, that's why the president is calling it that!

Grunt.

Mary was sure the xenophobic president wasn't calling it that just because of its point of origin.

"It's a bio-weapon that they created over there. And the masks they're selling us don't work against it. They know that! Heck, they probably soaked them in the virus before they even shipped them here, for all we know. I wonder if anyone has thought of that? Should I tell someone you think?"

Grunt.

Mary didn't know if she was getting nauseous from disbelief that one person could harbor so many misconceptions, or that it was due to low blood sugar.

"Well, we don't have anything to worry about here, thank God! Diseases like that 'China virus'", she accented with air quotes, "only strikes big cities where, you know, *those* people live."

No grunt this time. Apparently, there were limits to her husband's subtle encouragement. The loud spooning of his Jell-O paused momentarily, as though even he was taken aback by his wife's uncouth comments. She didn't seem to detect the change.

Mary, however, could feel the flush spread across her own face. James seemed lost in his phone, oblivious to the woman's monologue. Jesus just sat there, lost in his own thoughts.

The server arrived with their dinners just as the pair got up to leave. The woman walked by first, followed a moment later by her husband. He looked tired and resigned on his face. Mary's eyes met his, and he nodded to her, the gesture feeling apologetic. She nodded back, acknowledging the gesture, silently thanking him.

"We should hang around and watch them try to eat with those things on," Mary heard the woman say, but her husband shooed her towards the door and they were gone.

The trio bowed their heads, gave thanks, and dug in.

14 – Lena, Illinois

James slid the curtain aside and strolled the short length of the RV. The convertible bed on which Jesus had presumably spent the night, against his wishes, was back in its original sofa configuration as though it had never been used. He often admired Mary's tenacity, but not when he was on the opposing side, as he was in this case.

They had stepped away to discuss their options and after considerable debate, Mary had concluded that there was no other option; Jesus would have to spend tonight with them as there were no other accommodations available. James' offer to drive him into the nearest town, and even pay for the room, had rejected. No counter-proposal had been forthcoming. The long day had worn down his resolve, and he finally conceded to the arrangement, leaving Mary to handle the details.

James had then collapsed into one of the rear fold down beds and was asleep in minutes. Nothing had disturbed his slumber until a narrow shaft of dawn wiggled through a gap in the shades and fallen on his face.

Had Jesus chosen to find somewhere else to sleep? James shook off the mystery and staggered outside. The dawn, it seemed, brought some answers. Seated twenty feet away on the nearest picnic table was Jesus, attention fully on him as though he had been waiting for him to emerge.

James had pondered nodding a casual acknowledgement and climbing back inside, but he noticed Jesus had his hands wrapped around one of the turquoise plastic mugs, which gave off a wispy trail of steam. His nostrils pulled in the scent of dark roast coffee. Kenyan, if he wasn't mistaken. When his eyes spied a second mug on the table, resting at Jesus' elbow, any thought of retreat evaporated.

As though reading his thoughts, Jesus lifted the other mug and set it down across from him, enticing James to approach. It felt like a trap, but he brushed the logic aside and inched cautiously forward.

Taking the coffee without taking a seat seemed improper, so he sat down, asking with his eyes if the mug was for him, and received a silent smile and confirming nod in reply.

James pulled it towards him and breathed it in. So much potential, he thought, and took a tentative sip. Perfect temperature. Perfect aroma. Perfect roast. He wondered how Jesus had pulled it off, worried that he had broken the agreement and had started a fire to heat the brew. One glance in the fire pit next to the RV showed no such activity had taken a place in a very long time. He certainly hadn't used the stove top in the Winnebago to make it, James knew.

"How?" he inquired, more than a tinge of awe in his voice.

Jesus beamed, arms wide and hands facing heaven.

"Created the universe. What's a cup of coffee?" James added, having heard the story from Mary.

They sat in silence for several minutes before James felt the need to fill the silence, something he was loath to do but seemingly powerless to avoid. "Been up long?"

"Came out here in time to see the dawn. It's always a blessed event for me, each a unique gift. None of us know how many days the Father will grant each of us."

James preferred sunsets, the dawn arriving far too early for his taste. And today, he wasn't sure he was in the right frame of mind to start off the day with heavy, theological discussions. He wanted to let the observation slide by, unanswered, but felt strangely compelled to dive into the deep-end despite his own father's recent death still an open wound.

"I hope you're not going to tell me how many I have left."

"Would you even want to know?"

James shrugged, his father coming to mind again. "Some people might, particularly as they get older."

"Possibly."

They said that alcohol loosened lips, but the coffee he was drinking seemed to have a similar effect, inhibitions waning. "I think my father would have wanted to know. And mom," he said, his voice trailing off. James could feel the unfamiliar, long-buried emotions well up inside him once again. It had been a while since had experienced them.

"From the cancer?" Jesus confirmed.

James' pity party was pushed aside and their eyes met, a sense of pain being shared. Mary must have told him, he concluded, but couldn't fathom why she had felt compelled to even mention it to Jesus.

"Yes." he confirmed. "At least we were there for her at the end."

Jesus looked on, his full attention on the man across from him. "That couldn't have been easy."

James laughed, but the sound contained no humor.

"Dad's dying was unexpected, but in a way that was a mercy. We had spent the better part of two weeks with mom in the hospice ward. And when the time finally came, and she slipped away, nothing happened."

James looked up at Jesus and could see tears in the man's eyes that he knew mirrored his own. The man nodded in an encouraging way, as though he had experienced similar pain.

"The people working in the hospital continued to scurry past her room. Cars outside kept moving. Folks on the sidewalk outside never paused. The most remarkable woman on the planet had just died, and the world didn't even notice; didn't bat an eye," he said sadly. "They didn't realize what they had just lost."

James pushed the memories back down inside himself and tried to close the bottle again. He wiped away the tears and cleared his throat, intending to change the subject, but he wasn't done yet.

"But I should have been there for dad," he said, the sense of failure palpable in his voice. "I need to help Mary finish this trip. I owe them both that much."

"No one is blaming you, James. Hospitals have rules in place right now."

"I know I couldn't have done anything to prevent his death, obviously, but he shouldn't have died alone, you know?"

"He was never alone, not for a second." Jesus reassured him.

There were doctors, nurses, other patients and a slew of support staff around at all times, but James knew deep in his heart that Jesus wasn't referring to the employees. At hearing those words, he felt some of the weight lift from his shoulders as though speaking of the pain to someone else meant sharing some of the load as well. He breathed deeply, the cool morning air calming him.

They heard the door of the Winnebago spring open and then shut again, foot falls coming up behind James. He swiped at the remnants of tears that streaked his face and didn't turn to face his sister when she took a seat next to him and wrapped an arm around him.

"Good morning," Jesus said, reaching down to his side and passing her a steaming mug of tea.

"Should I ask where this came from?" Mary asked.

James shook his head.

She sipped the scalding hot tea with gusto, enjoying the burning liquid as it sliced vertically through her chest. Then Mary paused, the mug hanging in her hands, just below her nose. Her eyes shifted to Jesus, as she drew in the floral steam, the notes of bergamot, piquant, and vanilla, chillingly familiar. He smiled at her, eyebrows raised, and took a sip of his own tea, lifting the mug in a silent toast.

Mary swallowed hard, memories flooding back. It didn't happen often, but smells could often trigger some of the most intense memories. She had serious doubts that James could even recall her favorite tea, much less having mentioned it to Jesus in passing, but Mary would swear that the cup in her hand contained the magical brew that mom used to whip up for them.

"Who's wants breakfast?" James asked suddenly, jumping up and disappearing inside the Winnebago without waiting for an answer. A moment later, the engine turned over, breaking the early morning silence.

15 – Stockton, Illinois

The first signs of civilization along their route, west on US-20, appeared ahead in the windshield. The goldfish crackers that Mary had finished and washed down with the last of her tea, wasn't holding her over, so they opted for a drive-thru breakfast on the run.

This morning the line was short, and they got to the window without incident, greeted by a cordial teen who looked far too young to work there. The staff was fast and efficient, and the trio quickly had their order. Mary confirmed it, passed Jesus his grub, and they were off again, running along the two-lane ribbon of asphalt.

Traffic was light and the speed limit was a comfortable fifty-five miles per hour, but they still had vehicles pushing them hard from behind. They plowed ahead at the fastest speed the sturdy Winnebago could muster.

When Mary looked back, Jesus was eating his eggs and potatoes, a smile on his face.

"Hash browns are another gift from the Father," he murmured, between bites.

The road stretched out ahead of them, small towns whipping by.

Woodbine.

Elizabeth.

Tapley Woods.

Galena.

Exactly an hour after grabbing breakfast, the Mississippi River appeared out the left window. The sun was up, it was a beautiful morning, and the temp high enough to have the windows open, the smell of fresh air flooding the camper.

"Is this Heaven?" Mary asked, as they drove across the bridge spanning the famous waterway.

"No, it's Iowa," her brother replied, quoting from one of their favorite movies.

They all laughed, enjoying the moment.

16 – Dubuque, Iowa

Crossing the bridge, their luck ran out, traffic grinding to a halt. In the distance, they could see a traffic light, but there were also a lot of pedestrians milling about in the roadway, mixing in with the cars and trucks. Picket signs being waved, even from fifty yards away, were clearly visible.

"Do I have to lock the doors?" her brother teased.

"Depends on the issue," she answered, her eyes and interest on the scene ahead. James would not have been surprised if Mary asked him to pull over so she could fab a quick sign of her own and join the folks lining each side of the roadway.

Many of the drivers, it seemed, were interested in what was happening ahead and were in no real hurry to make it through the light. A camera crew from the local news station was setting up, and the police were standing by to monitor how things progressed. So far, other than the mild slowdown, the event here seemed far different from what they had left behind in Lansing. It clearly had a different vibe too, they both thought, when they finally inched forward and got their first look at the crowd.

Protests. No counter protests. Scanning the signs on her side of the road, Mary picked up all the latest topics: *Constitution, Freedom, Rights, Violation, Sweden.*

"Bingo!" she called out; all the latest themes present.

Scanning the opposite side of the street, she saw it was much the same. Protestors and not a single counter-protestor in sight. They were actually witness to a rally, she surmised.

"Want to stretch your legs?" James offered.

"No thanks," Mary replied, not really feeling it.

"You've never let a one-sided fight stop you before," he said, in a way that seemed like a compliment. It was true, she knew. That there were seventy-five of 'them' and would be only one of her hadn't been an obstacle in the past. Mary wondered how the local law enforcement would respond if she were to step out and challenge the crowd. She smiled a bit at the thought of how it might all go down.

"I know. Just don't have the fight in me this morning," she replied.

Mary looked back to find Jesus quietly watching their exchange.

"But standing up for what's right is never the wrong thing to do," she added, never taking her eyes off of Jesus, who nodded, clearly in agreement.

"Most of them have demands. But at least one guy has a good point."

Mary turned back as though someone had slapped her.

"Which guy?" she questioned, looking out her window for a clue.

"Sweden guy."

"What about him?"

"They didn't go on lockdown and things have turned out okay."

"Have they?" Mary asked, as though trying to trip up a witness on the stand. "How so?"

"Their society is wide open and things haven't crashed."

"Their death rate is three to ten times higher than that of its nearest neighbors, who have locked things down," she quoted from memory.

"Really?"

Mary nodded and continued. "Sweden also didn't consider that the younger citizens have jobs and some of those folks work with seniors and nursing homes."

"Oh, no."

"They've really let their seniors down. For the younger population, the virus has burned through with minimal damage. And they've had a higher infection rate than most countries, but have paid the price. We could have done that here too, but it's not that simple."

"How so?" James asked.

"Everyone there has health care. Those that became unemployed during the pandemic didn't lose their health benefits. And from the beginning, the Swedes took this seriously and minimized their exposure through proper social distancing and the wearing of masks in public."

"Voluntarily?" he asked, surprised.

"Yes."

"I'm not sure that would have worked here," he admitted, knowing the penchant in the US for not being dictated to, even under such trying circumstances and for the greater good.

"Employees there have paid sick leave, so they don't have to choose between staying home sick and not getting paid. Too many people here in the states feel that they have no choice but to go to work, even if they're not feeling great and might be infected. And they *do* still have restrictions in Sweden, such as limiting gatherings to fewer than fifty people."

"Wait, they have some restrictions in place?" he asked, wanting a clarification.

"Yes, they do. And their citizens have voluntarily isolated themselves and kept their distance. The population is also one of the healthiest on the planet."

"So, it's not the rosy picture it sounds like?"

Mary shook her head, wishing more people did their homework rather than latching onto a soundbite and slapping it on a picket sign.

"Afraid not. You saw what happened in Michigan; hospitals around Detroit nearly overwhelmed. And that was with the emergency order in place and businesses shut down. Health issues and other factors play into that, but can you imagine what would have happened if we had let things stay open? Or if people from metro Detroit could travel back and forth between their cottages up north?"

"It would have been a mess," he admitted. "Can't be more than a few ventilators in those areas and hospitals are rare."

"Medical facilities aren't designed or staffed to treat most of our population at the same time. Not even a fraction, actually. No way for any society to maintain facilities for such infrequent events like this pandemic."

"Flattening the curve," James said.

"So that the number of sick people doesn't exceed the capacity that the hospitals were designed to support. Only so many beds, so many ventilators, so much medication available. It's not like you can call up a staffing agency and have them send over fifty thousand doctors and nurses on a moment's notice."

James sped up the Winnebago up to its top speed and left Dubuque in their rear-view mirror.

17 – Peosta, Iowa

"Is it wrong to have ice cream before lunch?" Mary asked, digging deep into her sundae. Cones couldn't contain enough toppings and forced you to eat far too quickly. She had learned over the years.

Jesus, from his perch in the back, was enthusiastically shaking his head, a thin bead of chocolate syrup running down his chin from his Peanut Buster Parfait.

"Not if it *is* lunch," her brother tossed out in their defense, wincing from brain-freeze.

When Mary looked back again, Jesus was pointing at James with his spoon, clearly in favor of his answer.

"This is inspired," Jesus mumbled to himself, scraping fudge from the sides of the cup.

After they finished, Mary thoroughly rinsed the containers before she recycled them and tossed the rest in the trash.

"I've read a lot, but there must have been protests in your day," she asked, taking a seat on the bench. It might have slipped by his sister, but James' interest was piqued when he detected the insinuation in her choice of wording.

"Oh yes. There was always discontent bubbling up someplace. But these out here?" Jesus said, waving his hand toward Dubuque, "Aren't really what you would call a protest based on my experience."

Intrigued, Mary asked. "How so?"

"Well, one, no one died," he said, ticking off the count on his fingers. "Two, no one is going to be fed to the lions. Three, no one had their property confiscated. Four, no one even got a ticket, much less was imprisoned, locked in chains, and tortured. And five, no one's job, career, or way of life was seriously at stake. In the past, you put a lot more on the line if you were going out to fight for someone or

137

something. Because of the potential dangers involved, people knew you really meant it when you stepped out to challenge authority."

"I guess we don't really protest then, when you define it that way."

Jesus shook his head.

"That back there? In my day, we would have called that a party."

Mary laughed. "It looked like that, didn't it?" she said, picturing the crazy outfits and all the smiles.

"If they truly feared for their lives, would any of those people have been out there?"

She didn't have to ponder the question for very long. "No way."

"And if you have nothing to lose, you're just frustrated. Maybe showing up with other people who are like-minded and equally frustrated allows them to vent those frustrations. But those folks who showed up in Oregon this week? They all had different agendas and were just looking for a stage on which to perform. Free advertising when the news cameras roll and cell phones publish pictures to social media. That's what they really crave now, attention, not true dissention."

"But what about the cause?"

"Irrelevant," Jesus said. "You know the old expression that, 'they're just looking for an excuse'? It's the same here. Not a new thing."

Mary wondered if that's why she did what she did? Was she just looking to be seen? She deflated slightly at the potential revelation.

"It's not," Jesus commented, catching her eye, when her gaze drifted up to him again. As though reading her mind, he continued. "Like you, some people truly believe. They have a passion that drives them. Publicity is not their motivation. Those kinds of people will risk something for a fight and for injustice. That is what real protesting looks like."

It was as though he was not only talking to her, but about her. She felt the hairs on her arms stand up, a chill running through her. In his words, she found motivation.

Jesus said, "Interestingly enough, most people wear masks at protests where they think the authorities might identify them. Today, you would think more people would hide their identity, but they don't. If they wore masks, their friends on social media wouldn't know that they had even attended these events unless they posted their selfies on Instagram. No one would recognize them in the videos broadcast by the local news organizations unless they posted their own videos on Facebook. No, most only crave the publicity and self-promotion, believing incorrectly that their actions are for the greater good."

Mary nodded, knowing how much easier it was to stand out in the cold, heat, or snow when there were others standing by your side and when you truly believed in what you were doing. "Not a fan of social media?"

Jesus made a rare scoffing sound, clearly not looking happy. "God gave us all the gift of intelligence and this is what the world does with it? It's bad enough to shameless self-promote yourself as false idols, but what does it say about people who waste their lives watching crazy videos and pranks? Don't get me wrong, I love cats, but aren't there more valuable things you can do with the limited time each of us is given?"

She understood, somewhat embarrassed, that he was probably, again, specifically talking to her.

"But have you seen the one where the cat is like a goal keeper?" she asked, acting like she was kidding, but really wasn't. She watched that clip a dozen times a day.

He smiled at her, not saying anything.

"So, no redeeming value to social media?" she asked.

"The Internet? The military originally developed it, so I guess using it for cat videos is potentially harmless. And during times like this pandemic, social media allows for churches to get the Word out to world without risking in-person services. Charities can reach more people and be more effective. Schools can operate safely.

"But on the flip-side, it provides far too many avenues to spread hate, divide communities, waste time, drive lies, and ruin lives. The Internet has taken the good and the bad and amplified it all. While it's drawn some families closer together, it's driven others apart. Things that someone wouldn't say to your face are posted instead, often anonymously, for the entire world to see. It's made society far more efficient at being good or being evil. It just depends on how it's used," he concluded.

"Too bad it wasn't around back in your day. You could have tweeted all kinds of mean things about the Roman oppression."

Jesus smiled, a mischievous glint in his eyes. "John the Baptist would have loved it," he had to admit, a kind of melancholy passing over him.

"You started a few protests, too," Mary commented.

James hadn't tossed anything in yet, Mary noted, but she was sure he was listening intently to their exchange.

"They didn't call that time in the temple a protest," he acknowledged with a smile. "Other terms were used, some not so nice."

"What about the gatherings going on now? They're challenging the decisions of our leaders."

"Well, the people also wanted a king, remember, and our Father gave them what they think they desired in their hearts. They learned soon enough that He knows what's best for his children. He often answers such prayers knowing it will provide a painful lesson, but it's never done out of spite, only love, because He is always there to help carry those who believe in Him through any trouble. It's not always pretty, but He never lets an opportunity go to waste."

"It is better to note the protest of the wise, than for a man to give ear to the song of the foolish," Mary quoted from memory.

"Ecclesiastes. Nice." Jesus beamed proudly, impressed.

"A friend of mine begins each day by quoting it, and shaking her head, as we set up our counter protests," Mary added. "I guess one man's wisdom is another man's folly."

"There is only one source of truth, but not everyone gives it heed," Jesus reminded.

They both shifted slightly, feeling the RV losing headway.

"Gas stop," James declared over his shoulder, in way of an explanation for the change in momentum.

All three climbed down and did the obligatory stretching, something familiar only to those that drive or ride for long stretches of time.

While James pumped and Mary shopped for snacks, both watched as Jesus slipped on his mask and drifted away towards a man at a neighboring pump who was leaning against his car, gaze distant.

"Does he know him?" Mary asked, when she returned with a grocery bag in each hand.

"He technically knows everyone, doesn't he?" James asked, more than a subtle dig in his tone which Mary hadn't detected before.

When James made to reach for the tube of Pringles that was poking out the top of one bag she held, Mary pulled it brusquely away, stepped aboard, stowed their treats for later and then, in a sign of her disapproval, climbed over the center console, and dropped into the driver's seat, belting herself in place.

"Fine. You can drive," he said, climbing into the passenger seat, grunting as though it took great pains to sit on the other side. She knew her brother had control issues, and it was good to set him straight occasionally. Besides, she thought, his attitude could use a timeout.

They watched out the driver's window as the man at the pump stepped forward, social distancing be damned, and snatched up Jesus in a big bear hug. At least he also had a mask on, Mary noted. The man didn't appear to want to let

go, but eventually felt awkward and released Jesus, who

stepped away, bowed slightly, and returned to the

Winnebago.

18 - Dyersville, Iowa

The trio were standing shoulder to shoulder, each experiencing something different.

"Isn't this outstanding?" James said, breathless, his eyes wide in awe, a goofy grin plastered on his face.

"It is." Jesus agreed.

Mary scanned the entire area, strangely devoid of people, and came to a different conclusion.

"I don't get it." She might as well have punched her brother in the guts, all the wind driven from his sails by her lack of enthusiasm.

"What don't you get?" James asked, flabbergasted, arms waving at the historic scene laid out before them.

"Historic," James declared in this weird, 'David Attenborough' sort of way.

"Historic," she repeated, more as a statement than a question.

"Yes, historic! All the things that have gone on here," he clarified, turning back to survey the scene as though he were overlooking Normandy or Gettysburg.

"They shot a movie here," Mary commented flatly.

She might as well have stabbed James, the way he deflated before her eyes.

"Not just any movie, for heaven's sake!" he declared, then realizing what he said, turning to Jesus. "No offense."

Jesus shrugged and shook his head. "None taken."

It baffled Mary, not understanding the appeal.

"A baseball flick. It's like Kevin Costner's fifth best movie," she continued, yanking his chain now for amusement.

"It's his *best* movie!" James challenged. "*Field of Dreams* is a classic! It's even on the Library of Congress' National Film Registry."

"That was shot here?" Jesus asked, looking around with a new appreciation.

"That list can't be *that* great," she said. "*Empire Strikes Back* is on it too."

If there was one subject that was more forbidden to critique than James' obsession with *Field of Dreams*, it was anything 'Star Wars' related. Mary must have scored a direct hit because her brother looked flummoxed, unable to speak. "And granted, the second movie wasn't that great and the fourth movie jumped the shark, but how can neither the original, nor the third Indiana Jones movies be on the list if it's so comprehensive?" she pondered aloud.

Her brother might have had a thing for Star Wars, but she was an Indiana Jones girl.

"Okay then," James turned towards his sister, not willing to concede the point. "Which Kevin Costner movies were better than *Field of Dreams*?"

"There's *The Guardian, Hidden Figures*, the Superman movies," she went on, trying to pull up from memory what other movies in which the actor had appeared. "*Waterworld.*"

"Oh, c'mon now, you're just making this up," he said, declaring his verdict. "No way *Waterworld* is better than *Field of Dreams*."

"Alright, maybe not *Waterworld*," she conceded. "But what about *Dances With Wolves* and *Mr. Brooks*?"

James nodded, a crack appearing in his resolve.

"I forgot about *Mr. Brooks*. That was a pretty good movie, too."

"Oh, and *The Bodyguard*."

She knew she was piling on now, but she couldn't help herself.

James grumbled a bit, clearly not appreciating her arguments.

When Mary started laughing, the gag was up and James, who looked like he was going to kick her a moment ago, started laughing too.

He looked around one last time, trying to soak in the experience, then took an obligatory selfie of him and the ball diamond behind him. "Let's go. I'm getting hungry."

As they walked back to the RV, Mary turned to ask what Jesus thought of the place. "You liked it too?"

"Oh yes, but not for the same reasons."

When James looked at him wounded, Jesus added. "Although I really liked *Field of Dreams* too."

"What did you like about it?" she asked.

"On the glorious splendor of your majesty, and on your wondrous works, I will meditate," Jesus replied, quoting Psalm 145:5. "The Father works his miracles in large spaces," he said, nodding to the colorful afternoon. "Yet even at the smallest scales, his genius is undeniable.

From the wavelengths of light that reach our eyes to even the arrangement of the kernels growing on the corn in the outfield. All of it is part of the Father's intended design."

"Wow," Mary and James exclaimed in unison.

"There are always flowers for those who want to see them," Jesus added.

"Bible verse?" she asked, unfamiliar with it.

"Henri Matisse." he laughed. "The Father inspires so many."

19 – Manchester, Iowa

Pizza was something you never tried to eat while driving. Mary knew from far too many previous failed attempts. Instead, they called in their order, and told the owner who took the call, that they were setting up their own dining space in his parking lot.

They pulled out three chairs and one of the small folding tables they had squirreled away in the RV. Plates, napkins, and fine-dining plastic wine glasses completed the ambiance that she was aiming for.

Mary had already relinquished the rest of the driving that afternoon to James, so she retrieved and opened their only bottle of wine, a Spanish Txakoli which was her favorite. She twisted off the screw top and poured Jesus and herself each a healthy serving.

They were soaking up the sun for another fifteen minutes before the pizzeria owner wandered out, hands and apron still dusted in flour.

"I put it into a box in case you had any left to take with you," he said, setting the pizza down. Mary salivated at the sight, the curled pepperoni holding little pools of meat juice and grease.

"It looks amazing," they all commented, much to the delight of the owner, who looked very proud.

Despite setting up in a parking lot, it did nothing to dampen the outside dining experience under the brilliant sky. She would have to do it more often, making a mental note.

Before they dug into the cheesy pie, the owner produced his cell phone and held it up.

"Would you mind?" he asked, pantomiming as though he were already taking a picture. "It's for our customer wall inside."

"Of course," Mary replied, before her brother could toss cold water on the man's simple request.

They all turned and posed for the shot, a mix of emotion clear.

"Thank you so much for your business," he said with just a hint of an accent. "Everything OK? Need anything else?"

The trio shook their heads, surveying their lunch.

"No, thank you. It looks marvelous," Mary replied.

The man bowed in a graceful, old-world sort of way and retreated inside.

"Would you mind saying grace, James?" she asked, when the time came.

He raised his head slightly and spied her out of the corner of his eye. Mary had already bowed her head and clasped her hands in front of her, waiting for him to get underway. Jesus, likewise, was doing the same. James licked his lips and gave himself a moment to gather his thoughts and search his memory for the right words.

"Ahh, Dear Lord, we thank you for this food we are about to eat and for the love and grace you always show us. Amen!"

"Amen," Jesus and Mary added, before serving up the pizza.

They ate in silence for several moments before James spoke up.

"So, Jesus, the guy you were talking to back when we filled up with gas?" James asked, in his usual passive-aggressive way. Mary studied her brother for a few seconds, wondering where this was going, before turning towards Jesus, herself curious.

Jesus nodded, as though reliving the experience. "He lost his father a few weeks ago. Blames himself for the death. He was sure he had the virus and when he thought he was over the infection, he went back to helping his father, who lives on his own. Although he had no symptoms, he was still sick and believes that he gave it to his father."

"Oh my God," Mary exclaimed, a wave of nausea pushing her appetite away. "I can't imagine what that would be like."

James grabbed another slice; not sure he had wanted to hear the answer to his question after all. It was striking both of them too close to home, having lost their own father to COVID less than a week ago. Could only six days have passed since they had been in his hospital room? The cavalier attitude he showed then seemed inappropriate now.

"He's not sure?" Mary asked.

"No. The cause of death was a heart attack, he told me. And back when it happened, they didn't know all the ways this virus presents itself. He's been tested, and doesn't have the virus. And the tests to see if he had it aren't available yet. He believes his father is dead now because of him and it's affecting his relationship with his mother, who has her own health issues and also lives alone."

"And you convinced him it wasn't his fault?" she surmised, given the man's reaction.

Jesus nodded, stuffing the final bit of crust into his mouth and finishing his glass of wine. "Nothing happens without the Father, who determines our steps and how many we're granted. He's no more responsible for his father's death than anyone else here," he waved at a family coming out of the restaurant, heading for their SUV without masks on. "But he notes of those who live their lives without considering others."

"Is he going to be OK?" she asked, as her brother got up abruptly, folded up his chair and walked away. She eyed his departure, but Jesus seemed unphased.

"Yes. Both him and his mother are both going to be fine," he reassured her.

"Our own father didn't take the virus that seriously, but he stayed home a lot more when the orders came out. We're not sure where he picked it up or how long he had it. We didn't see him much since the emergency started. Both of us were afraid that we might get him sick."

James dropped by when their dad needed his help occasionally. Mary was beating herself up for not having been there as often as she could have.

"You both did great," Jesus said. "He was lucky to have you."

Mary smiled, tears threatening. She knew there would be times like this when she would feel overwhelmed by the feeling of loss. It was only natural, and it helped to heal the broken-hearted as long as a person didn't allow the grief to paralyze them. Experience with losing her mom taught her it would happen eventually, following the loss of their father.

During the weirdest of circumstances and the most inappropriate of times, Mary would feel the tears and anxiety coming on. It really was only just her and James now, with a few other family members to call on, most living out of state. Jesus' blessed assessment came at just the right time.

"Ready to go?" she asked, knowing that getting back on the road would be a welcome distraction from her introspection.

Jesus nodded, while James crushed the empty pizza box with a bit more fury than was needed and tossed it in the can outside the restaurant's front door. He stored the small table and chairs before climbing back behind the wheel.

The pizzeria owner poked at his cell phone in all the right places, as his grandchildren had taught him several times to do, the gratifying sound of the small photo printer in the pizzeria's back office reaching his ears. He retrieved the photo and wandered back into the foyer of the restaurant's entrance, where he stuck it to the faux-wood-paneled wall with a bright blue pushpin.

The man studied it for a moment, confused, thinking back and trying to remember the scene, but lost his train of thought when movement outside drew his eyes away, the retreating motorhome shrinking into the distance.

20 – Waterloo, Iowa

By the time they reached the eastern edge of Waterloo, Jesus was already leaning against the inside of the RV, a comfortable breeze blowing across his face, asleep.

Mary confirmed her suspicions via a quick look over her shoulder and then broached the sensitive subject that had been nagging her for quite a while.

"What's up?"

He didn't answer right away, continuing to stare through the windshield as though he hadn't heard her.

"With what?" he asked, looking at her way in a detached sort of way.

"With you. You seem pissed about something. Did I go overboard back there at the Field of Dreams?"

"No. That was fun, actually. A pleasant diversion. Thank you," James said with a chuckle.

"Then what is it?"

James was pissed, but not entirely sure why. He hated that feeling, shrugged, and went with the truth.

"I am, but I'm not entirely sure why."

"Is it Jesus? You seem to direct most of your comments in his direction."

"I dunno. Maybe. That guy at the gas station. He," James said, thumbing over his shoulder towards their slumbering passenger. "Convinces the guy he had nothing to do with his father's death, when he could just as well have been the one who infected him."

"But you heard him. Jesus said he didn't," Mary defended.

James rolled his head and his eyes, then stared at his sister. "He's not Him, you know," he stated with conviction. "Which means he has no way of knowing that to be a fact."

"Okay. Let's assume he's not Him," she conceded.

"Let's assume he's not? Listen to yourself, Mary. You can't still be entertaining that possibility, can you?"

She didn't answer yes, but didn't deny it either.

"Assuming he's not," she continued, "Jesus just walked up to a total stranger, who, by his own admission, was overwhelmed with guilt that he likely contributed to his own father's untimely death. A man who was now so paralyzed by fear that he was struggling to help his own mother. With a few encouraging words, whether they were true, Jesus enabled the man to live again. To be a person who serves his mom, and presumably others, who will now be even more aware of the dangers that the virus represents and will take all the precautions to ensure those around him are safe."

"It's still a lie."

"Possibly."

"Probably."

"Potentially," she defended. "Certainly, no more than a small, harmless, white lie."

"All lies are bad," he said, quoting Mary from many of their past conversations that had ventured into some gray areas.

"In this case, and some of those you're now referencing, I might have been incorrect."

"Wrong?" he asked, smirking.

"Incorrect," she laughed, before turning serious once again. "No harm done, only good. Nothing could or will ever be proven either way. Being released from his guilt, the man can move on from this tragedy. And he clearly won't become more ambivalent towards the potential danger the virus represents, but more respectful of the danger."

James chewed on the argument, clearly not liking the taste of it, but Mary was right. What if either of them had been in the same situation with their own father and been forced to shoulder the guilt?

"Maybe they were just talking about the weather, for all we know," he argued.

"And the guy smiled and grabbed a total stranger in a bear hug because it was sunny out?" she chuckled. It was clear, though, that her brother remained unconvinced. This was serious, she could tell, and laughing at anyone in that state never had the desired effect.

"Maybe it was a really long winter here," he countered, not even cracking a smile at the absurdity of the response.

"We didn't cause dad's death either," she added, seeing a parallel here. Both of them had regrets at his swift demise, but neither having seen him in the two weeks before his death they had not been at fault. A small blessing, she acknowledged sadly.

He nodded, knowing the truth in her statement.

"I know that," he replied, realizing that it had been a few weeks since he had been in his father's immediate proximity.

"Then what's the issue?" she gently probed.

Mary watched her brother physically struggle through the pain.

"Where is God in all of this mess?" he finally blurted out, getting closer to the crux of the matter. It wasn't the first time they had broached this topic, nor would it be the last. It was the biggest sticking point that most people had with the loving God that was at the center of Christianity. Why aren't people living flawless lives once they go all-in with their worship and commitment to Him?

"He's here," she assured him, despite it always being a hard sell. "Always with us. You know what mom and dad used to say. In our fallen world, we'll always have troubles. God doesn't want our obedience because He takes all those things away from us. He uses them for good, in ways we'll never be able to figure out. But He always carries us through the pain."

"God didn't heal mom though," he stated bitterly, shooting Mary a pained look. "No matter how much we prayed." James turned and focused his attention back out the windshield. Mary could see her brother was opening up, emotions flowing. This was a good thing, but never easy. She would be in the same state right now, but remembered her own advice that it was probably best that only one of them should lose it at a time.

She nodded, knowing it had been a hard time for him.

"Mom was healed, James. It just wasn't in this life," Mary said, shifting over between the front seats and wrapping her arms around him.

21 – Berlin, Iowa

The silence was broken when James, still looking at his phone as they sat in the rest area parking lot taking a break, started chuckling and looked over at Mary.

"What?" she asked, suddenly paranoid.

"Going to read you a quote and you have to tell me who said it."

She nodded, willing to play along. Her brother could be obtuse occasionally, but it was often harmless.

"'We have more cases than anybody in the world.' referring to viral cases, 'But why? Because we do more testing. When you test, you have a case. When you test, you find something is wrong with people. If we didn't do any testing, we would have very few cases.'"

That really hurt Mary. Like physically caused her pain. The level of disbelief beyond belief. She had hoped that such statements in the past had been misquoted, or at the very least misinterpreted, but no, there were far too many examples for that to be the case.

It also didn't help that once called out by the press and clarifications requested, the president would double-down on whatever bizarre notion he had said or tweet that he had sent. Continuously rotating spokespeople would just parrot the lunacy and defend the remarks no matter how absurd. It was sad for those sacrificial victims who voluntarily manned the White House podium, but more so for the Office of the President and our country at large, she thought. So much damage to be undone.

James didn't bother to ask for her answer because the question had really been rhetorical all along.

"You're killing me," she said, acknowledging the pain.

"I thought you couldn't get enough of this stuff," he replied, smiling widely.

Perhaps this was payback for her *Field of Dreams* commentary, she wondered?

"It's not that I can't get enough, it's that I can't stop reading it and get too much," she clarified. "And stuff like that terrifies me. It should terrify you, too. It should terrify everybody, frankly, but so many people just eat it up without so much as giving it a second thought."

"This comment even had me laughing. A writer named Quinn Cummings, in response to the president's remarks, wrote, 'Remember kids: You don't want a baby? Stay away from pregnancy tests!'"

Mary chucked. "That's pure gold."

"But her comment didn't appear on the president's Twitter feed, so it's probably deep-state, radical-left, socialist, propaganda," he added, parroting the president's frequent defenders.

She nodded, agreeing with his assessment.

22 – Fort Dodge, Iowa

They were making great time and were continuing, more or less, in a westerly direction. Save for the occasional bathroom break, food stop, photo op, or local attraction, their progress continued unabated. Mary had even found her groove behind the wheel from time to time, her normally insistent brother having divested his interest in driving.

"Check it out," he said, motioning ahead of them with his chin.

Pulled from her reverie, Mary's gaze followed his lead and landed on the only thing in sight, a billboard sprouting up in the middle of a cornfield lining the highway.

"'Aren't all businesses essential?'" she read aloud.

"What do you think?" her brother asked, expecting to get a rise out of her since he thought he had a pretty good read on where she stood on the topic. But she didn't immediately bite, watching the ribbon of road ahead while pondering the sentiment.

"Tough one," Mary conceded, clearly struggling. "It's such a mess right now in all the states. I'm not sure any of them have gotten it right."

Instead of the playful fight he had expected, James noted her solemn tone and struck a more conciliatory note.

"Without federal guidelines, they forced the states to come up with plans on their own, which is pretty screwed up. I mean, that's the purpose of the federal government, isn't it? For something like this?" he asked.

"Won't get any arguments from me on that one, James, you know that. Complete breakdown. Definitely not a ten out of ten as the president has scored his own administration's performance."

"I certainly can't come up with much in the way of a defense. It seems like the CDC wants to do the right thing, but their hands are tied," he said.

"You're right. Unfortunately, their proposals are only recommendations at this point and the administration is leaning on them to support the president's narrative. Election year, so it's only natural, even if it means more people are likely to die because of it." Mary's eyes darted to the rearview mirror, wondering if she might get Jesus' opinion on their discussion, but he was still snoozing comfortably in the back.

"I'm struggling with the sentiment that the billboard was proposing," he said. "To the person who owns that business, and its employees that rely on it for their income, it's probably essential."

"That's why we have unemployment, isn't it? There is the additional federal compensation too for those out of work. And the stimulus package, which has only been a single, onetime payment so far, but there are other social programs in place to assist with temporary shutdowns."

"More darn socialism!" James declared, at least partially in jest.

"Yup, those darn socialists keep trying to infiltrate our government with their free handouts," Mary replied with a smile. That was another topic they had debated considerably in the past, so it was an inside joke shared between them.

"The administration has been talking about cutting the additional funds back early, instead of letting the additional federal program expire. Apparently, people who have to live on minimum wage are making more now by simply staying home, and it's dissuading them from returning to their workplaces."

"Staying home, staying safe, and not infecting others," she clarified.

"Well, many of them aren't staying home. Once the courts have overruled some of the governor's restrictions, people deemed it open-season on summer. Didn't matter if there was a threat or not, they apparently thought the virus posed no risk, and the legal orders were no longer in effect. I've seen videos from all over. From the Ozarks in Missouri, to Chicago here in the Midwest. Birthday parties to grad parties. And the authorities, even if they acted, no longer have the authority to do so. Many sheriffs are choosing to ignore any orders, which they've decided on their own, to be unconstitutional."

All the videos Mary had seen were disappointing. Were all the precautions for naught? Would these 'spring-breakers' carry the virus home or were they all locals? Maybe they were right, she considered. Most of the fatalities were the elderly, trapped together in nursing homes, cared for by people who were forced to take multiple jobs in multiple facilities just to make ends meet.

Had some states chosen to throw caution to the wind and allow their citizens free rein to risk exposure? Sure.

Had some states gone too far the other way in some cases? No doubt.

'Too far' wasn't a right term she took lightly. It reduced the deaths and allowed the hospitals to cope, but had the orders gone on so long now that the gains were no longer being realized? Had the economic damage exceeded the cost in lives? How much was a human life worth exactly? she wondered.

They would write about this historic event, and discuss it thoroughly on college campuses, for decades.

Then Mary focused back in. "Many of those folks on spring break will go home and they'll take the virus with them, not understanding the negative impact they're going to have on their families and communities. Most will live on blissfully unaware of the people they've infected or, God forbid, killed. Strangers dropping and no way of tracing it back to their poor judgement and behavior. Can't imagine what it would feel like if a family member of theirs dies and they're likely to have been the cause. We saw that with the guy at the gas station. I'm not taking any chances at being that person. And I don't care if I get grief over wearing a mask and using hand sanitizer."

"I hear you, sis. You would think, though, that there would be a standard list of what was and wasn't essential in an emergency. Hospitals and grocery stores, you need. Often manned with minimum wage folks who have to deal with angry customers and potentially getting sick. There are auto-mechanics that have to keep cars running for essential employees like hospital staff, police, and fire departments, but does that mean they can't work on other people's cars? Is auto-detailing essential or do they have to reduce their offerings? What about home improvement stores? They allowed them to stay open to sell appliances, but they had to close their lawn care centers, much to the consternation of people who bitched that they couldn't buy plants for their yards. Memorial weekend was still two months away, and we were still under frost-freeze warnings in Michigan. Then there were the barbershops," he said, leaving the last item on the list hanging there for her.

"Don't get me started on that topic," Mary begged.

"But then the bowling alleys and tattoo parlors could open. And although I know the president doesn't have the authority to do it, he was pushing for the gyms to reopen, remember? I have a membership that I never use, so it can't be that essential, right?"

They both laughed.

"Don't forget, he had a visit from an influential supporter that week, who owns a string of gyms. It pays to have access. Or is it that having access pays?" Mary asked.

The people who say there is privilege, but it doesn't provide an advantage for anyone in our society, clearly have privilege but are too immersed in it to recognize it, she thought.

"And don't forget about the churches," Jesus added, suddenly appearing right behind them.

"Jesus!" James blurted out, jumping at the man's sudden appearance.

"Yes?" Jesus replied, smiling.

"That's a big one," Mary conceded. "Don't suppose you have the answer?"

"It's all about sharing your faith, not your space. What greater love than to give up your life for another? A close second would be sacrificing your desires, not necessarily your life, to protect others by staying isolated and taking the precautions. That's how you love and serve. If churches, or mosques, or other spiritual gathering places think they are doing their congregations a blessing by needlessly exposing them, then they're actually doing them a great disservice. If the doors are open, many people will feel compelled to attend, even to the detriment of their health or the health of others. If they want or need to stay home and spend that time reading the Word, the Father won't hold it against them. God knows the hearts of man and will always provide."

"That's a nice thought," Mary said, swinging off the highway.

"Not a thought," Jesus reminded her. "A promise."

"We could have put the money they spent on a billboard we saw a few miles back to much better use," she concluded.

"Hallelujah," Jesus replied.

23 – Early, Iowa

"According to Wikipedia, 'Early, [Iowa's] claim to fame is that it is the Crossroads of the Nation, because Iowa Highway 71 and US Route 20 intersect there," James said, consulting his phone as he leaned against the side of the RV.

Mary had reminded him enough times about cell phone use and gas pumps, so he made sure he was both sufficiently grounded and far enough, in his estimation, from the nozzle.

"And it wasn't just incorporated 'early' in Iowa's history, it's actually named after one of its first citizens," he continued.

It wasn't a large town, Mary noted, but the gas station this afternoon was crowded. Jesus, after speaking to a few passing travelers, seemed to meander aimlessly around the parking lot.

"Bill, strange things are afoot at the Circle K," she said, laying on the accent to go with the movie quote.

James turned, familiar with the quote, scanned the area for the source of her comment. It didn't take long to find what, or in this case who, she was referring to.

"I knew it wasn't just a water sport." James replied, also from the same movie.

They watched as Jesus, off to one side, arms straight out, had a flock of small birds jockeying for prime positions on his outstretched extremities.

"Wouldn't make a very good scarecrow," he noted.

"Nope," she acknowledged. "But what's attracting them? Doesn't look like he has food on him. You remember the Bible saying anything about birds?"

James shrugged, silent at first, not sure he wanted to feed his sister's growing obsession, but eventually played along. "Other than the creation story in the Old Testament?

Not really. Gospel of Thomas has a story of Jesus creating birds from balls of clay," he added, buttoning up the fuel cap.

"I always forget about the gnostic texts," she said, referencing the gospels that hadn't made it into what would eventually become the King James version of the Bible.

She wasn't surprised that James could pull up the reference, as he used to be very in tune with his faith. The death of their mother had certainly been the final straw for him too, but his active participation in worship had already been waning for some time, for reasons she had never fully figured out.

As if on cue, all the birds flew away and Jesus returned. He seemed at peace, even here at a humble gas station. Maybe that was the key to happiness, being able to find joy anywhere you found yourself. She would have to ask him later how he managed that feat.

"Ready?" she inquired.

"Always." Jesus replied with a smile.

24 – Correctionville, Iowa

"It looks like they're open," James commented, perusing his phone.

"Mind if we call it a day? I'm ready to stop for the night," Mary asked.

James agreed. He had had more than enough for one day.

"Ready to stop, Jesus?" Mary inquired.

"Absolutely," he replied.

Mary suspected he would have been just as happy to keep going. He always seemed content, an outlook that she desperately desired to possess. 'Oh, the places you'll go! There is fun to be done!' she whispered, looking at him in the rear-view mirror, seeing that his gaze was upon her. He smiled, nodding as though he had heard her quoting Dr. Seuss.

"We have anything to barbeque?" she asked James, who nodded. "If not, we can get Jesus to conjure up something."

James had grown quiet, not bothering to respond, eyes still on the phone in his hand.

Mary slowed the RV as they came into the small town and were approaching what looked like the main light in Correctionville, Iowa.

Is there a prison nearby? she asked herself? With a name like you would almost have to think so. If not now, then it probably it did in the past. She shook off her butterflies, trying to concentrate on the last miles of their day.

"Left," James offered, when it looked like Mary was going to blow past their turn. She did as directed and followed the narrowing road south, deeper into town.

"And it's *not* named after a prison," James offered, as though he had had the same thought.

The butterflies must spread, she pondered with a smile.

"According to a local paper, *The Courier*, quoting the city's website, 'Surveyors, in making land divisions, used correction lines. Since the world is round, every land division from North to South cannot be the same size because the earth curves toward the top. To allow for this, East/West correction lines were established, and adjustments were made along those lines to make all land parcels nearly equal in size.'

"That's cool. Logical too, I guess," Mary said.

"The article continued by saying that, 'Since the city's central East/West street, Fifth St., was laid along such a correction line, the city was named after the practice. Because Correctionville's North/South streets follow the adjustments of the correction line, they all have a jaunty little jog at Fifth St.'"

As if on cue, Mary slowed at the light, noting that they had no straight route forward. James consulted the map on Google and sure enough, the road jogged as noted by the newspaper.

"Right," he said, noting the light change. "And then a quick left."

"The article wasn't kidding. Fifth street here on the map looks like a fault line has slid out of place. All the streets that run north to south across fifth street, have the same discernable jog that the newspaper mentioned. Birch Street, Driftwood Street, which we're on, Fir Street, Hackberry Street. Strange."

Mary nodded, swinging the RV around the next left and back onto its southerly course.

James gave her the new heading and then continued with his observations.

"North-south streets are named after tree species. East-west streets are numbered. Angled streets are avenues. Seems orderly."

"As though there was a plan and a planner?" Jesus inquired, appearing again behind them.

"Obviously," James answered, but only Mary picked up on Jesus' inference. So much in life looked as though it had been well thought out and organized by a designer, like their talk earlier about wavelengths of light and even the humble ear of corn.

The campground appeared in front of them.

"Looks like we made it," Mary commented, more than ready to climb out and quit moving for a while.

They drove in and parked outside the office. Mary and James masked up and stepped inside.

The woman behind the counter threw up her hands and spoke as though terrified, despite wearing a wide smile. "Don't hurt me. I'll give you whatever you want," she said, mocking their mask wearing.

Mary and James both turned their heads like a pair of confused puppies. Mary caught on but her brother, still confused, just let it go.

"Reservation number?" The woman asked.

"Sorry, we don't have one," Mary replied, noting there couldn't have been more than a half dozen sites occupied when they had driven in.

"Good for you! Most folks from out of town usually have them. They don't enjoy venturing out without having their ducks in a row, know what I mean?"

Mary wasn't sure if she should have been insulted by the stereotype, or happy to have been, apparently complimented for not being overly organized. She could feel her mouth screw into a weird shape, which would have conveyed her displeasure, but the mask on her face had saved the moment from becoming awkward.

James paid for the night and they prepared to leave when several popping noises went off.

"Fireworks?" he inquired.

"No, that's the gun range next door. Don't worry though, they'll be finishing up soon."

James looked at the woman, dubious. Some of those reports sounded pretty large.

"What time do they close?" Mary asked.

"They don't really have a closing time. They just have to quit once it's dark, since there aren't any lights installed on the range."

"Told you I should have brought my AR," James added, signing the check-in form and elbowing his sister.

Mary noted that the woman behind the counter seemed to appraise her brother in a more positive light, having learned that he was a gun owner. She enjoyed going to the range with James occasionally, but the fascination, which bordered on obsession with firearms, had troubled her for years. Having that kind of power in your hands could be an adrenaline rush, she knew, and a stroke to the ego. But the answer she often received, on why people in cities owned guns they couldn't hunt with and only shoot at the range, was simply because they could. It seemed unnecessary, she supposed. And despite firearms leading to daily tragedies, there didn't appear to be a rational way out of the dilemma. The genie, they said, wasn't going back in the bottle.

She always interpreted the second amendment to mean that the right to keep and bear arms shall not be infringed upon, until a well-regulated militia, for the defense of the nation, would take over that role. Others, though, clearly didn't, and would never, see it that way.

Even having domestic terrorists shooting up elementary schools full of children, on what seemed like a regular basis, wasn't enough of a motivation to move the country forward towards some kind of sensible gun reform. The lobbyists were earning their paychecks, and the politicians kept sweeping up their hefty campaign contributions.

They found their assigned lot, no neighbors tonight so far, parked and were hooked up in minutes. They fired up the grill and dropped on some steaks, while the fresh corn boiled. The reports echoing over from the gun range kept going off, but their frequency was diminishing, just as the woman behind the counter had predicted.

"There's a gun range next door," Mary explained to Jesus.

He nodded, but in a way that gave her the impression he already knew. Then she remembered his axiom; 'created the universe from nothing, remember?' So, it should have not surprised her that Jesus would know exactly what those sounds represented. Or that he would know what she thought, every minute of her life. Or that he knew exactly what was going to happen to each of them tomorrow. It was both unnerving and comforting.

Mary noted that as the first fireflies flickered to life, the final few reports from the gun range died away.

"Another miracle," she said, her eyes transfixed by the glowing insects. They had always seemed to be, even to this day, a source of magic to Mary.

"They're everywhere," Jesus replied. "With every breath we take."

"Every move we make," James added.

"Our Heavenly Father will be watching you," Mary concluded.

They all laughed, eating a wonderful meal. And enjoying a wonderful evening, Mary realized, only because their father had passed away and James had agreed to help in fulfilling his last request. A twinge of guilt distracted her. If their father had gotten better and been released from the hospital, he'd probably be at home alone right now, microwave dinner on a folding table set up in front of his television playing reruns of Hogan's Heroes or Magnum P.I. He was old school like that, she thought, reminiscing.

Would she and James have fully appreciated how close they had come to losing him? Would they be at his house right now eating and watching television with him, trying to spend every second they could with their father, knowing that they had all just dodged a bullet?

She let the thought drift away, not wanting to fully reveal the answer. Mary knew better, though. They might have given thanks he had beaten the illness, but she was under no illusions that their respective lives would have really changed all that much.

"Why can't we fully appreciate moments like this?" she pondered aloud, not really expecting an answer.

"Why can't we appreciate any of the days that we've been given?" Jesus countered. "Pope Francis said, 'Gratitude is a flower that blooms in noble souls."

Mary looked over at the brother, who looked angry, sad, tired and tipsy, his eyelids drooping heavily. He drained his beer bottle and then stood up suddenly, declaring his intentions.

"I'm going to bed." With that, he turned, stepped ten feet to the door, and disappeared inside.

"I'm sorry, Jesus. I'm not sure what's gotten into him," Mary said in the way of an apology, pissed at her brother on her own behalf. She was about to go after him, but Jesus gave a subtle shake of his head. Mary looked at him and then at the camper's closed door. Making a choice, she settled back into her seat, poking at the last of her steak. She turned and held out her plate, offering Jesus the rest. But again, he shook his head.

"No, thank you. I'm full," he said, patting his belly. "And thank you again for the lovely meal and for letting me share in your adventures."

"You're very welcome."

"And don't be too hard on your brother, Mary. We all grieve in our own ways and he's struggling, as are you."

She smiled, but it wasn't one of joy. It was one of those fake, placating smiles you slap on your face when you're hurting, but someone asks how things are going?

"I'm fine," she said, mimicking the popular, societal response, when someone clearly isn't doing well. If the person asking doesn't know you well enough, they can't see through the half-hearted effort. But she knew, even if this wasn't *the* Jesus sitting not more than five feet from her, that he could see right through her false façade and straight into her heart.

Maybe he was a passing preacher, who intimately knew the Word? Maybe he was an unemployed chef, down on his luck? Maybe a doctor or surgeon who had buckled under the stress of the pandemic and was wandering the country trying to find peace?

Maybe he was God?

She couldn't bring herself to ask again, for fear of the answer she might receive. She was worried he might deny it. Or was she actually worried that he might confirm it and that she wouldn't have the faith to believe it? Far too many folks in the New Testament, who knew of the signs and should have recognized the Savior when He appeared in their midst, either failed to see what was revealed, or had chosen not to see it. Would she be any different? Better to maintain the status quo, she concluded.

"Some of the world's greatest wisdom comes from the Father down through His prophets," Jesus began, knowing she was still worried about her brother. "Many still go old-school and receive His wisdom from books, but many more receive His knowledge through movies."

"Movies?" she asked, baffled.

"Sadly, few people pick up books these days. They associate them with school and when their formal education ends, they don't see a need or have a desire to go back to the written word. So, our Father has turned to the movies, or television, and other means as well. He'll use any method to reach His children."

"This isn't all leading back to *Waterworld*, is it?" she asked, laughing nervously. Mary often turned to humor, she knew, to shield herself in times of stress, a revelation that hadn't come early or easily.

"Oh no. I was thinking of *The Best Exotic Marigold Hotel.*"

"It's one of my favorites!" she declared, but for the life of her, she couldn't remember any quotes from the movie that might be of biblical proportions.

"It will all work out in the end. If it hasn't worked out yet, it's not the end," Jesus quoted from memory.

Mary had watched the movie a dozen times and could even picture the scene, but until this moment, she had never picked up on the quote or its relevance.

"He works miracles every day. God didn't do them just so they could be recorded by the Apostles, Mary. And like the Word of the Father, He's still spreading it today, just in ways that people wouldn't expect."

"I didn't pick up on the importance of the quote before," she admitted, feeling bummed at the implications.

"Nor should you have," Jesus defended. "People turn to the Bible and His Word, but often it doesn't stick with them. At different times in their lives, under vastly different circumstances, the Word conveys only then what they need to know. Don't ever feel bad for reading the Word, and not being able to relate to the message. There are so many interpretations and meanings depending on the experiences of the reader and timing."

"Makes perfect sense."

"That's also why it may be profoundly impactful on you, while the person in the pew down the row might seem distracted and are daydreaming. It blew away you and they failed to pick up on the subtle nuances that week."

"Or vice versa," she admitted, relieved that some weeks, when she attended services, it failed to feel relevant.

"Exactly," Jesus confirmed.

"So, it will all work out, in this world or in the next?"

"That's right, just like you told your brother earlier today."

"You heard that?"

He nodded, smiling. "I don't miss much."

Like many people, she wasn't sure she would have been as confident speaking about the Word with James if she had known that Jesus had been listening in. It was silly; she knew.

"You did great," he added, studying her more intently as he asked her the next question. "Why is it you can speak out with such passion when you witness an injustice, but when speaking of God and the Word, you hold back?"

Mary hesitated, knowing that they had just moved into a very sensitive topic in her life. They were going deep.

"It's just us," Jesus encouraged, with a grin. "Pretend I'm a priest and you're confessing."

She chuckled nervously, stalling. "I'm not Catholic."

"That's okay, neither am I," he said. "Be honest. Your brother is asleep and there isn't another soul around," Jesus added, waving his arms in all directions.

Mary took a deep breath and nodded, looking around before she began.

"Okay. When I see an injustice, I just seem to snap. Not in a crazy sort of way. Usually, I just start moving to set things right before I think about what I'm about to do. But when I'm speaking about God, I often have more time to think about what's coming and doubt creeps in. I feel unprepared, I guess, or not qualified to speak about such things."

"Who would be more qualified to speak about your relationship with the Father than you?"

"Priests, pastors, nuns, theologians, philosophers, fortune cookies?" she said, rattling off the usual sources of God's wisdom.

"Granted, yes, many are gifted speakers and they spend more time in the Word, but you have the same access to your relationship with God as they do."

"You're talking about my testimony?" she asked.

"More than that," he assured her. "Plenty of smart people have the Bible memorized, but it's how the Holy Spirit works within us to interpret the Word. And just quoting scripture doesn't impress people. In fact, it often intimidates them. You, Mary, impact so many more people by your actions, through loving and supporting others, than you ever could by simply quoting scripture."

"'I'd rather see a sermon than hear one any day.'" Mary replied, quoting the poet Edgar Guest.

"There you go. Show people you care and they'll follow you. Maybe only on Facebook, but it's not up to you to change their hearts." Jesus laughed, pointing at her. "You're just providing an opening for the Lord to do His work."

Mary smiled, proud and pumped up. Jesus was right, of course. "More adventure awaits us tomorrow, I suspect," she said, rising to her feet, ready to turn in.

"I hope to arrive to my death, late, in love, and a little drunk," Jesus quoted.

"Pope Francis again?" Mary asked, laughing.

"No," he said, joining in. "Atticus. An oldie but a goodie."

"Have a good night, Jesus."

"A blessed night to you too, Mary. Thank you both for a wonderful meal and for sharing your evening with me."

25 – Correctionville, Iowa

Mary awoke first, to birds chirping and then to the sounds of gunfire. Unfortunately, it wasn't an unheard-of combination in her life, her own neighborhood going through painful renewal.

It took a moment to gather her thoughts and figure where she was and what she was hearing. As per their routine, her brother was still asleep, logging long hours as he had when he was a teenager. He could fall asleep in moments and stay that way for hours on end. Age, apparently, had not affected that talent.

While there were many things pushing her to stay in bed, a delicious smell wafted through the Winnebago, and her stomach provided a stronger argument to get up and face the day.

She padded her way outside, not having seen Jesus on the convertible bed, and found him seated next to the grill, the large, family-sized, cast-iron skillet laid across it.

He smiled and poured her a cup of her fragrant tea, piping hot, like she preferred it. Heaven, she thought to herself, as she unfolded a chair and sat down next to the grill, the warmth helping to revive her as much as the caffeine. She sipped the tea, still groggy. Mary was sure now that it was the same tea that she and her mother had enjoyed, but was afraid to confirm its identity with Jesus. Perhaps, she wondered, it was just such a popular blend and a coincidence that he liked it too.

"What's on the menu for today?" she asked, leaning in, heading for safer territory. Deep philosophical discussions would have to wait until she was fed and fully alert.

"Veggie omelets with a side of hash browns and grilled catfish filets," Jesus replied, plating the food and passing Mary her plate. She said grace for them and eagerly reached for a fork.

"I've never thought of having fish for breakfast," she admitted, studying the beautiful presentation. Could she picture Jesus working as a chef in a New York restaurant, which lined Central Park? Watching him work with skilled precision anything was possible, but the longer she was with him, the harder it was to picture him living in such mundane circumstances. His cooking, though, was delicious.

"Did you ask the fish to swim up to you?"

He looked at her with a sly smile and raised expectant eyebrows, but didn't answer, so she did it for him, nodding.

"Created the entire universe out of nothing. How hard would it be to make to a fish come to you, etcetera."

He smiled.

"What is that outstanding smell?" James asked, stepping out of the RV. He seemed like a different person from the night before. Something she noted was not uncommon with most of the men in her life. They could go to bed, fall asleep in seconds, snooze through the night, and awake the next day as though the events of yesterday had never happened. Daily reset, Mary called it. While she, and many of the women in her life, were not so lucky. They accumulated daily worries like it was baggage and found it difficult to divest it again.

Still looking half asleep, Jesus handed him a plate and James took it gratefully, not bothering to even sit down.

"I've never thought of having fish for breakfast before," he said, mirroring his sister's sentiment. "What kind?"

"Catfish," Jesus replied.

James looked at his sister. "Did we pick up catfish?"

Mary shook her head, exchanged a knowing look with her brother, and motioned with her cutlery towards Jesus.

"Actually, the folks over there," Jesus nodded up the way, "lent me a fishing rod and the creek provided."

Mary looked a bit disappointed following such an ordinary explanation.

While James was engrossed in his meal, Jesus extended his hand towards Mary and held it there, eyes locked on hers. Mary stared at his fist, pondering for only a few seconds this time, before obediently placing an open palm under his. When he opened his hand, another gold-colored Sacagawea, US $1 coin, tumbled into hers. He winked, and they shared a conspiratorial look. The implied miracle did wonders for her soul, while the more mundane explanation probably worked best for James, given his agitated state last evening.

"You should open a restaurant, Jesus. This is delicious," James offered, studying the enigmatic man for signs of a reaction. Mary, while peeved at her brother's duplicity, was curious as well, her gaze also watching.

"Me? A restaurant?" he said, staring off towards the rising sun, light flickering through the trees. "No. That doesn't sound like me, though I do like feeding people."

The sounds of gunfire broke the spell as another day on the range signaled another day on the road for them. They packed up and climbed aboard.

26 – Sioux City, South Dakota

Four hundred miles on US-20 finally ended. It wasn't unexpected, but still sad, Mary noted, with more than a hint of surprise. It had become familiar, like an old friend, albeit one made of concrete, asphalt, and steel.

Up ahead, the passage from Iowa into South Dakota seemed subdued compared to their arrival into Iowa from Illinois. It could have been because of her brother's excitement at visiting the *Field of Dreams*, but she felt downright apprehensive about leaving the Hawkeye state behind. They were one state closer to their destination, and they still didn't have a plan on what they would do when they got there. It had been left up to her, and she had been avoiding all thoughts of its eventuality. Until now, she frankly wasn't sure they were even going to get there, but progress had been steady.

"Want me to take a detour so we can say we made it to Nebraska?" James asked from behind the wheel. He remembered the games they used to play on trips, wanting to check off as many states as they could. She smiled, still tired from another restless night, and shook her head.

"Not unless you want to."

He didn't particularly want to, so they continued on.

"I could pull off, over there," he said, pointing to a thin spit of land protruding into the water.

Mary looked over, but saw no reason he would want to.

"That's where South Dakota, Nebraska, and Iowa meet," James clarified.

"Doesn't look like public property," Mary said.

"It's not."

She waved him off, no longer considering the side trip. "No thanks. Trying to avoid being arrested today."

"Why just today?" he inquired, knowing her protesting past had provided for some previous detentions but no serious charges. She gave him a disapproving look, but was smirking at the same time.

"Funny."

The wide expanse of the Missouri River, visible off to their left, with Nebraska just on the other side, disappeared behind them. The Big Sioux River, taking its place, with South Dakota now on the opposite side. A minute later, the Winnebago crossed the bridge, which signaled that they had formally entered 'The Mount Rushmore State'. Leaving both waterways behind, they continued north, a darkening bank of clouds filling the entire width of the windshield.

As the miles rolled on, James, not one who enjoyed quiet time, flipped on the radio, hoping to fill the void. The dial landed on a local station that was carrying the daily presidential briefings. Although it would have been wise to let the experts from the CDC pass along the data, it was the president who often took to the podium and presented his

own thoughts on the pandemic.

"A lot of good things have

come out about the Hydroxy,

a lot of good things have

come out. And you would be

surprised by how many

people are taking it,

especially the front-line

workers, before you catch it.

The front-line workers,

many, many, are taking it. I

happen to be taking it. I

happen to be taking it. I'm

taking it.

Hydroxychloroquine. Right

now, yeah. Couple weeks

ago, I started taking it.

Because I think it's good;

I've heard a lot of good

stories. And if it's not good,

I'll tell you, right? I'm not

going to get hurt by it. It's

been around for forty years,

for malaria, for lupus, for

other things, I'd take it.

Front-line workers take it. A

lot of doctors take it. Excuse

me. A lot of doctors take it. I

take it. I hope to not be able

to take it soon, because I

hope they come up with some

answers."

In almost comedic fashion, and without taking his

eyes off the road, James' right hand drifted to the radio knob and switched it off before sliding back into the two o'clock position on the steering wheel.

Mary, looking stunned, opened her mouth to speak, but nothing came out, and it closed again.

"That was weird." James acknowledged for them both.

Mary was speechless, but after considerable effort, words finally spilled out.

"I'm not sure what I just heard there, and which part of it amazes me more. That the president says he's taking an unproven drug to prevent the coronavirus, or that his doctors in the White House, who should follow the science and know better, are allowing him to take it?"

"Maybe his doctors are giving me a placebo? You know, to placate him?"

They both started laughing hysterically.

"That's brilliant, James! Can you imagine the scandal if that ever got out?"

The moment passed though, and things turned heavy again.

"But seriously," James began. "These drugs have been around forever, right? They're basically safe."

"True. Both of them are relatively safe, but there's not any real data on their safety when used in combination. And despite the president's remarks, there's no evidence yet that they're even effective against this virus. Studies were started, but some were cut short because of unexpected deaths and other complications. It's certainly not something you want to take on your own outside of medical supervision, I understand," she said.

"And if people were interested enough before to try it as a prevention drug, when the president was only pitching is as a potential panacea, imagine what's going to happen now that he says he's actually taking it," he added, pointing at the radio.

"It's scary that it has potential, deadly, side effects, but the president has twenty-four-hour medical staff within feet of him at all times. No way that anyone else at home should take it, the CDC said. And it's not like these two drugs are impossible to get. Doctors prescribe z-pacs all the time. People probably have some lying around in their medicine cabinets. And if they know someone who has lupus, they have easy access to the other. This is just crazy," Mary said, shaking her head in disbelief.

27 – Sioux Falls, South Dakota

They found a promising spot and climbed out, stretching, a dark sky and misty rain falling. They hurried towards the building, which featured a small café, moderately filled with people, but few were eating or drinking.

"Start without me. There are some folks here that I need to see first," Jesus said, stepping back into the drizzle.

Mary and James continued on. As soon as the pair walked in, they were pegged for the outsiders that they were, suspicious glances turning their way. No hostility, just a wariness that Mary seemed to detect.

One server showed them to a booth along the front window and handed out menus.

"Passing through?" the woman inquired, a bit more loudly than was necessary.

"Yes," Mary said. "How did you know?"

"It's the masks."

Curiosity got the better of her and the look on Mary's face communicated that fact better than she could have ever voiced in a question, so the woman continued.

"You don't work at the plant, which means either you're management from the plant or you're just passing through town. And since you're wearing masks, I assumed the latter."

"Management from the plant wouldn't come in here wearing masks?"

"They almost never come in here and if they did, they most likely wouldn't be wearing masks, no," she clarified. "Besides, since this whole pandemic thing started, the managers from the plant have mysteriously disappeared. They're all working remotely now, I understand. Stopped coming physically into the plant weeks ago when things started getting bad."

Mary nodded, unsure of how to respond. Interest in the pair faded once the server took their drink orders and retreated.

Looking around, everyone else had masks on, including the staff. Every other seat at the counter was occupied, something that hadn't likely happened on its own, and every other booth was open. It might not have been to spec, but given the state's lack of restrictions, she gave them a passing grade for their efforts.

The conversation, which had slowed to a murmur when they had entered moments ago, picked up again. Mary did not know what most of them were saying, given that she could detect several languages, and knew none of them.

"Waiting for your friend?" the server asked as she set down their drinks.

All three looked out into the darkening midday rain and spotted Jesus peeling off from a line of folks positioned under the awning across the way. He crossed the narrow lot, stepped inside, and sat down.

"Hola. Cómo está usted?" he asked the server.

The back and forth between Jesus and the woman, in what sounded to Mary like fluent Spanish, caught both her and James off guard. But should they have been surprised, she wondered?

By the time their exchange ended and they placed their orders, the woman's disposition no longer matched the weather outside. Whatever Jesus has said seemed to have turned things around, at least for a while. Many of those seated near their booth, in fact, were also smiling, having taken a fresh interest in Jesus and his two companions.

He had that way about him, Mary conceded. She looked at James, who was still studying his menu, seemingly oblivious to the change which had just transpired around them.

After the server had dropped off their lunches, Mary wanted to ask Jesus about the exchange he had had with the server, but a sense of heaviness had displaced the magic that had been present in the room. Even Jesus, immune to mood swings, had grown quiet and sullen as he picked at his meal.

"Something wrong?" Mary asked, noting a change in his disposition. Even James looked up when he realized that Mary's inquiry had not been directed at him, but Jesus.

"Remember what I said yesterday outside the market?" he asked, not turning to look at her. His eyes were slowly sweeping the small knots of people seated inside the café, each lost in their own thoughts.

She nodded, remembering the young couple with the two small children who had wheeled their cart of groceries out while the three of them were still in line. Jesus had told them that the family would be fine and unaffected by the virus.

"That's not true here today," he replied, turning his attention to the server when she approached.

"Mas aqua?" she asked, but didn't take his glass.

"Si."

The young woman smiled again and stepped away, returning a moment later with a clean glass of ice water.

"Could I?" her brother began, raising his own glass towards her, but she had already moved on.

Mary didn't know if she still had an appetite, but continued to poke at her stack of pancakes, pondering the implication of Jesus' remarks and studying the surrounding faces. Who might he have been referring to? Certainly not everyone in here, she hoped. Such a gift, if it could be called that, had to be a heavy burden to bear.

When Mary's eyes finished sweeping the café and had returned her attention to their own booth, she found James gazing at her, silent. He wasn't studying her so much as glaring at her.

"I'm going to pick up some things in the market next door," he said, pushing his half-eaten breakfast away. "Looked like they could use the business and there wasn't anyone lined up outside. Can you grab breakfast?" he asked his sister, slipping on his mask, and leaving before she even answered.

She nodded, but he was already gone.

"Would you like me to get it?" Jesus asked.

"My treat," she said quietly, preoccupied by what had just transpired. It wasn't hard to guess.

"Thank you," Jesus said, sincerely touched by her and James' continued generosity. He got up, slipped on his mask, and began walking around the cafe, speaking with the various groups scattered about. Mary watched as he moved from table to table, always keeping a respectful distance.

The government here, like many other places, was actively ignoring the evidence, or was failing to grasp the credible threat that the outbreak represented. In viral hotspots like the local meatpacking industry, things had already gone from bad to worse. The president's executive orders, which shielded the industry from many legal issues, acted more as an incentive to keep the lid on the deplorable conditions, and were not intended to help keep the outbreak contained and employees safe in the workplace.

'It's the way they live,' the politicians kept hammering to the press, trying to lay the blame for the outbreak at the feet of the employees, often immigrants from Central America and Africa. The same employees who worked in cramped conditions for only a few dollars more than minimum wage. To make ends meet, they were forced to share apartments or squeezed themselves into rented houses. Most times, the employees had no choice but to accept housing from their employer, which packed workers into dormitory-style environments.

After the president provided cover for the plant's owners, through legal liability protection via the Defense Act, the owners had very little incentive to enact any real safety protocols in their facilities. Instead of spending their valuable resources on making the environment safer for their employees, they chose instead to spend them on lobbying the CDC for exceptions to the workplace guidelines.

Many of the recommendations, such as slowing down the line, spacing out workstations and shifts, were all but ignored in the name of production and profit. There had even been threats that employees who failed to report for work, even though were exhibiting COVID-19 like symptoms, would be replaced. There were many lined up to accept the work that others had lost.

"So sad," she mumbled to herself, noting the folks outside trying to remain safely spaced out while huddled under the awning to stay dry. Even the weather, she noted, was trying to beat them down, but they looked like they were holding their own. Good for them, she thought, as she slid out of the booth.

Mary looked up when she heard laughter. Jesus was at a table, speaking with an older couple seated there. For at least a few moments, their problems were forgotten. The pair nodded to him and waved as Jesus stepped away, coming back in her direction.

Mary paid the bill, cognizant of leaving a healthy tip for the staff.

"Gracias," Mary said to their server.

"De nada," she replied.

Mary was filled with a heady swirl of emotions, ranging from sadness to anger to hope, as she and Jesus stepped back outside into the cool morning air. The rain had diminished again to just a sprinkle as they walked towards the RV.

"Thank you for that back there," she said, as they crossed the parking lot. "It really seemed to make a difference."

He nodded and shrugged. "Do you mind if I ride up front for the first leg this morning?" he asked.

She would normally have had no issue with giving up her seat to Jesus, but James' angry departure only minutes ago gave her a moment's pause before answering.

"Of course," Mary replied, climbing in the back this time.

James was already behind the wheel and had the RV fired up, ready to go.

"Get the groceries?" she asked, trying to see if his temperament had improved.

He simply nodded over his shoulder so Mary could see it. Then he looked at Jesus for a moment before shifting the RV into gear and pulling away.

"Can we make a quick detour?" Jesus asked.

Mary held her breath, wondering how her brother would receive this request. To his credit, James simply nodded, waiting for further instructions.

"Just up the road, in that direction." Jesus pointed.

As they pulled away, Mary could see that two small passenger vans had rolled up in front of the café and people began piling in, social distancing no longer an option. Her heart sank at the potential repercussions.

Minutes later, and a few miles down the road, an immense building came into view. The two vans had quickly caught up to their RV and the three of them were headed in the same direction. When James turned the Winnebago, the vans turned. Ahead, Jesus directed James to pull in and park near the gate. The vans also turned in but drove further forward, the passengers spilling out and merging with a much larger group already assembled in the parking lot. Shift change, Mary assumed.

"Thanks. I'll be back in a few minutes," Jesus said, climbing down.

Mary took his place up front, watching Jesus, as he had back at the diner, began moving amongst the small knots of people, exchanging words. He looked so at ease as he worked from one small pocket of employees to the next, many smiling or crying as they conversed.

Providing spiritual guidance and comfort was something she knew all Christians were called to do, but she never felt confident enough to put it into regular practice. She used to help at church occasionally and with various charities around town. If a friend or family member needed something, she was always there. Even having encouraging words for passing acquaintances at work was something she had no trouble doing. But approaching and sharing her faith with a complete stranger? That was a scary proposition. Did she feel like a complete fraud because she didn't know God's Word well enough to speak to others about Him? Maybe this trip would provide just the needed boost in confidence she needed to do what she was called to do.

"Looks like we should be good on groceries for the rest of the trip," Mary commented, referencing the large group of bags stacked on the floor in the back. "Thank you for picking those up."

"They had some great deals," James replied coolly, as Jesus wrapped up his ministry and headed back in their direction.

Mary started to move, but Jesus motioned for her to stay where she was.

He climbed in the back and took his usual spot. "Thank you," he said, pocketing his mask and sanitizing his hands. "I wanted to catch them before they started their shift."

Mary could see the mass of humanity slowly drift towards the entrance, many lingering, trying to keep their distance. They wouldn't be so lucky though once they reached the locker rooms or their workstations.

"Ready to roll?" James asked, studying Jesus in the rear-view mirror. He nodded, so James navigated the RV towards the freeway.

"West and north, or north and west?" he asked his sister.

"Have a preference, Jesus?" she asked.

When he shook his head, she turned to Siri and inquired. Without a specific destination, though, the phone app was of little help. Scanning the tiny map on her screen, it was literally a coin toss. The shortest route to the Montana state line was north and then west, but to get to the area around Yellowstone, the only famous place in the state she could name, was almost a straight shot to the west. Mary knew she hadn't thought this completely through yet. Until now, it had all been a purely theoretical exercise. Yellowstone still sounded right to her.

"Make it so," she said, pointing west, trying to sound like Jean Luc Picard from Star Trek.

James chuckled, getting the reference, but laughing because it was such an awful impression. "Your Sean Connery is much better," he said, trying to lay on the appropriate amount of Scottish brogue.

She scoffed. "You have no grounds to mock my impressions after that pitiful attempt!"

Preparing to face the lengthy width of South Dakota, Mary tried the FM dial, finding little once they had left Sioux Falls in the rearview mirror. N.P.R.'s 'Wait Wait Don't Tell Me' ended and the news came.

"You sure you want to do that?" James asked.

"It'll be fine," she replied, confident that catching up a little couldn't hurt anything.

President declares that anyone who wants a test for the virus can get one.

States declare tests aren't available.

President reaffirms that anyone who wants a test can get one.

Experts acknowledge that access to testing is available in some places, but they're bad.

President declares vaccine by year's end.

Experts respond that vaccine is a year away.

President concedes that wearing a mask is probably a good thing, but he won't wear one.

Experts declare that wearing a mask should be a requirement.

Administration officials bow to the president and don't wear masks when visiting hospitals.

Same experts declare that wearing a mask should be avoided.

Experts declare again that wearing a mask should be a requirement.

Same experts declare that there aren't enough masks and only frontline, medical professionals should wear them.

Experts declare that there are finally enough masks, but they aren't sure if doing so is good or bad.

Some states declare businesses may open, but everybody must wear masks.

Woman in Flint, Michigan, dollar store refused business without a mask, despite her mother wearing one. Family returns later, shoots and kills the employee for doing his job. All four family members now facing life in prison after the cold-blooded murder.

James, without asking for permission, reached up again and turned off the radio.

"I've shopped in that store," Mary said, eyes staring straight ahead, words catching in her throat.

A mile passed in silence.

"I've probably seen that employee before," she continued in a whisper.

Another mile passed.

"That entire family of four woke up that day, free but under a simple stay and home order. And now all four of them are probably going to prison," she concluded.

Under normal circumstances, James would probably have tossed in a comment or two, but even he knew it wouldn't be well received at this point.

After the next mile passed, James finally piped up and looked in the rearview mirror, directing his question this time to Jesus, who seemed to follow their discussion with interest.

"So, what's the story, Jesus? Why does God let awful shit like this happen to good people who worship him?"

Mary heard the baited question, and the tone coming from her brother, but she was too tired and demoralized to chastise him for it. Besides, it was a question that often kept her up at night.

She turned in her seat, afraid at what she might find, but Jesus, although looking a bit more forlorn now, didn't seem upset by the inquiry nor surprised by it. When their eyes met, Mary could see a sadness in his eyes though.

"Even those who worship Him aren't guaranteed a trouble-free existence in this life," he began, clearly comfortable with his answer.

"So that dollar store employee did something wrong? He didn't pray hard enough? Toss enough in the collection plate, maybe?" James baited, the mocking tone from earlier now replaced with unbridled anger.

"It's not how His heart works," Jesus defended, calm as though discussing the weather, his eyes still locked on Mary's.

"He had the power to stop it though, didn't He?" she prodded gently, wanting to believe there had to be a rational explanation for the tragedy.

"Nothing happens without the Father," he admitted, the pain in his eyes still clear. "And before you ask, know that He uses all things for good, even something as horrific as this."

"The father of eight was doing his job and a coward shot him in the back of the head, in cold blood! How can this be used for good?" James demanded.

"I know it won't suffice, but we could never hope to guess the plans that He has for any of our lives," Jesus replied.

James exhaled loudly, disgusted, but not knowing what to say. This was one of the sticking points that had driven her brother away from the church and his faith. One that many people wrestled with.

"Now the man's family is left to pick up the pieces," Mary said, taking over. "They're not paying a price for God allowing their family member to be killed?"

She could feel her face radiating the heat, and the pain, and the doubt that she could feel churning insider her.

"You don't understand, Mary," Jesus began. "When things happen in this broken world, that people conclude are bad or evil," he said, holding up his hands to stop her objections, "people believe it is because of Godly retribution because they can't see the big picture and all the ramifications. But please, please believe me when I say that our Heavenly Father does not, and cannot, work like that. He only has the best in store for us, even if we can't see it right away or ever. And although you think they're being penalized, realize that He is always with you, carrying you through it all. Without His grace and mercy, the troubles and tribulations that you face in this life would be so much worse, so much more painful, so much more unbearable."

Tears flowed, all three weeping, but for different reasons.

Mary had caught the implications. All those times in her life when she felt God was judging her for the poor choices she had made, she had never stopped to think about the good that could come from it and that He had never truly left her. It wasn't a solitary time-out after all. He was always there for her, carrying her through every ordeal she faced.

Mary felt them decelerate and the RV dropping down the exit ramp. James swung the camper off the road and up to the gas pumps, jumping out only seconds after they had come to a complete stop.

Mary and Jesus stepped out, and she could feel him evaluating her. She felt like she was coming unglued and probably looked the part.

"I'm sorry about all that," Mary said. "I'm usually the one getting fired up, but my brother can get passionate, too. He's still fighting some demons himself, from losing our mother, and now our father."

"He's not the only one, is he, Mary?"

She shook her head, quickly admitting to her own issues. "No, I have some of my own that I'm wrestling with, too."

"Want me to exorcise them?" Jesus said, trying for a bit of levity. Mary took it as the joke it was and she laughed, feeling the tension inside her draw back into its dark corner. He seemed to know her better than she knew herself.

"No," she answered. "It provides him with motivation, he says."

"And you?"

"Same with me, I suppose," she admitted.

Jesus nodded, understanding.

"Need anything from inside?" she asked, slipping on her mask.

"I'm fine. Thank you,"

Mary rounded the RV and gave James a big hug, and exchanged a few words before she released him and walked towards the store.

Both men watched as Mary disappeared inside.

As though Jesus knew what was about to transpire, he waited there for James to appear from around the back of the Winnebago. He watched the man open up the rear storage hatch in the side of the Winnebago, pull out a beat-up duffle-bag, walk towards him, and held it out.

"I believe this is yours," he said, accusatory.

Jesus didn't acknowledge the statement nor did he take the bag, so James dropped it at his feet.

"That's how you caught up to us before, isn't it? You stowed away in there before we left the truck stop."

Again, Jesus remained silent.

Before James walked away, he had one more thing to say, digging deeply and shaking his head.

"Mary's been through a lot lately and she's just lost her father," he began, refusing to admit his own loss. "And her world has been upended by a virus that has affected everything in her of life, apparently in good ways that we're just too dense to see. And yet, when she met you, she seemed to change. She found hope. But we're off to take care of our father's remains, and I think it's probably something we should do, you know, as a family."

If Jesus was surprised by James' comments, he didn't show it. When all James got was a simple nod in response, he turned and went back around to the gas pump. After he capped the tank, he noticed Mary heading his way.

"Want me to drive? You never let me drive," she whined. He smiled, but it felt wrong.

"How about all day tomorrow?" he called back over his shoulder, heading inside himself to clean up and use the facilities.

"You promise?"

When he threw her his patented thumbs up, she was excited at the prospect of getting some more time behind the wheel of this beast.

A few minutes later, James emerged and climbed back into the driver's seat, starting up the engine.

"We can't leave yet," Mary said, looking frantic, motioning to the rear of the RV. If there was even a hint of his duplicity showing, she must not have noticed it. James, playing his part, looked into the back of the Winnebago, knowing full well that Jesus wouldn't be there.

"He wasn't inside," James stated, technically not a lie.

Mary was checking the mirrors, checking their own lavatory, and even on the back bunks. No luck.

"Ten minutes. Can we give him ten minutes, please?" she asked, eyes pleading.

He hesitated only a moment before nodding.

"Sure," he mumbled, earning a smile from his sister that felt more like a stab in the heart than the gratitude it conveyed.

The time counted down quickly, but still no Jesus. When it struck ten minutes, Mary's anxiety seemed to reach a new level.

"He's probably moved on, sis," he said, aiming for something conciliatory between 'he has better things to do' and 'he'll be alright'.

"You didn't see which direction he went, did you?" she asked.

He shook his head. Again, technically not a lie. James had stepped back around to the pump before Jesus had wandered off.

"Can I just take a quick look inside?" she asked.

"Of course," James replied, knowing he had to let her try, if only for closure.

She jumped down and jogged inside. It wasn't a big place and other than the back room and two bathrooms, there weren't a lot of places where a person could be loitering. Mary emerged a moment later, looked around, and then disappeared behind the building.

James was about to get out and go after her when she emerged from around the other side, unaccompanied by anyone. With fists on her hips, she carefully studied each of the cars and trucks in the parking lot, but Jesus was nowhere to be found. He could tell from the look on her face that she had transitioned from being concerned to now being veiled in a deep sadness.

The pangs of guilt continued to chew away at him as he watched Mary cross in front of the RV and climb back inside. Tears streaked her pink cheeks, but she stifled a racking sob that was threatening to emerge.

He didn't have the courage to ask if she was ready to go, so he swung the RV back into traffic. Mary was still looking around for Jesus until they reached the freeway and got back up to speed. They were a good twenty miles down the road before she felt in control enough to speak.

"We shouldn't have said what we did," she started up, out of the blue, head shaking. "I wouldn't blame him for leaving either."

James couldn't argue. He had gotten pretty carried away himself.

"It wasn't you, Mary, it was me," he said, but quickly added, when it sounded more like a confession than he would have liked. "I got hot back there."

She nodded. Anger was one issue they had both been struggling with since their mother had died.

"It's not like we were criticizing him," James said, trying to defend their actions and the outcome.

"Didn't we?" Mary asked, not so sure now.

"What do you mean?"

"What if he was, you know who?"

"You don't still think he really was Him, do you?" James asked, worried, pointing skyward. He had to be careful now, not to fire up Mary on this point while she was grieving Jesus' unanticipated departure.

"He couldn't have been Him, right? Made a paralyzed man walk again. Could bring comfort to a stranger with only a few words. Made fish suddenly appear out of nowhere. Teleported from one state to another," she stated, but couldn't sell it. It was crazy to think that Jesus, if he had returned to earth, would have come in such an unassuming and understated way. But hadn't he done that the first time around too?

"And what are the odds we'd be the ones he would visit?" James asked.

"Why not us? I could certainly use the help." No deceit there, she knew. She was a complete mess, and it felt like the entire world was crashing in on her from all directions.

"We both can," he admitted.

"Well, He created the universe from nothing, so why couldn't He be everywhere, helping everyone, at the same time?" she said, laughing in a way that clearly scared James, but she didn't notice. It was probably a good thing she wasn't driving, Mary concluded.

They rolled on in silence, consumed by their own thoughts.

28 - Plankinton, South Dakota

Nothing dramatic to see out the window. No music to occupy her mind. No Jesus to talk to. This entire trip had been a mistake, she thought bitterly to herself. What had she been thinking? Clearly, she hadn't thought this through and had let her emotions lead her astray.

Mary laughed to herself, shaking her head, drawing her brother's attention. They had ridden in silence for the better part of an hour, and the sudden outburst was disconcerting to both of them. *The* Jesus is always with us, she mused, but it didn't feel that way at the moment. It felt like the opposite, in fact.

Yankton.

Crow Creek.

Lower Brule.

Rosebud.

Pine Ridge.

Road signs along the freeway called out the miles ahead to reach the distant reservations. Mary wondered how they were faring from the virus. Self-contained regions, their isolation acting like a natural fire-break, were often a blessing during pandemic events like this.

Maybe the local news had some stories and would provide a much-needed diversion from her brooding, dark thoughts. Mary picked up the newspaper lying on the center console next to her and flipped open the front section. It didn't take long for her to regret it.

Despite the continued silence, James kept looking over at Mary, concerned by the changes in body language he was witnessing. She even seemed to breathe loudly, he noted, but kept that observation to himself.

When Mary balled up the newspaper and threw it behind her, James determined it was time to inquire. "Should I be concerned?" he asked, far more than half serious.

Mary took several seconds to calm herself before speaking. "I should probably just avoid all sources of news, social media, etcetera until next year."

"Locals up in arms about the lockdown?"

She grunted, clearly dismayed. "Just the opposite. The state doesn't have any kind of stay-at-home order in place."

"We had people protesting back home about the order, and they're protesting here because of a lack of orders from the state government?"

"Definitely not. The local tribes in the state had a few incidences of COVID, so they locked down the tribal land to keep traffic out. And by extension, the virus."

"Seems like a reasonable precaution," James said, nodding. "Those on the reservations are not happy about it?"

"No. They seem to support the efforts."

"But?" he prompted, knowing there had to be an angle here he was missing.

"But the governor is demanding that they open up and remove the checkpoints they've set up."

"Can he do that?"

"*She* apparently can't enforce it, but some local ranchers claim that they're being denied access to their land because of the roadblocks."

"Their properties are landlocked?"

"Doesn't appear that's the case. It's just less convenient for them to go around using other roads."

"If she doesn't have the jurisdiction, what's the rub besides some disgruntled locals?"

"The disgruntled locals, as you call them, are one, not Native American and two, they're wealthy and well connected."

James was starting to understand the issue. It wasn't new, unfortunately, nor would this be the last time that such issues arose.

"She's been negotiating for a while to get the checkpoints removed, claiming that people need to use those sections of road to get to where they need to go. No luck so far and the pressure's mounting."

"Public roads cut through the tribal lands?" he started, but held up a hand when Mary made to argue the point. "While acknowledging that technically, this all used to be tribal land."

"It's a mess," she conceded. "Hundred plus years of boundaries moving, expectations established, informal agreements made," she said.

"So, the state is doing nothing to shelter in place, the president's declaration has made facilities stay open, said facilities are basically asking for exceptions to any meaningful actions to prevent the spread of the virus, not dealing with the thousands who are already infected, threatening to fire anyone who doesn't show up for work, bad-mouthing them in the press saying their lifestyle has led to the spread of the virus, and forcing tribal councils to disband checkpoints which could prevent the spread of the virus because all of this stuff is inconvenient?"

"Pretty much sums it up," she conceded.

"That even sounds crazy to me."

"I agree," she said.

29 - Chamberlain, South Dakota

"Hungry?"

"Yes, but can we grab something from the drive-thru? I'm not sure I'm in the mood to make anything," Mary conceded.

He nodded, understanding. In the distance, they had caught up again with the Missouri River. He swung off the freeway, angling towards a small town at the bottom of the ramp that seemed to have a decent selection to pick from.

"Might pull off down over here and eat with a pleasant view of the river," he commented, noticing a few places to park down by the water's edge.

They found a promising place and James swung the Winnebago up the street and into the line of vehicles waiting to place their orders. Even before noon, the queue was nearly ten cars deep. They weren't the only ones choosing to grab and go, rather than dine in, it appeared.

"Guess they haven't closed the drive-thru yet, forcing people to risk going inside to eat," Mary grumbled, clearly not pleased with the state's apathetic response to the virus. What Jesus had to say about many of those folks back at the café still clung to her. People were being exposed, many who would later get sick or die, and it was because of a lack of responsibility by many governments and politicians. "I wonder where Jesus is right now?" she added.

"Dunno," he said, putting the RV in park, and jumping out, the move catching her off guard.

"Where are you going?" she asked, but he was already out of earshot.

Her eyes picked movement in the side mirror, James appearing near the back of the vehicle on her side. He opened, peered inside for a moment and then closed a side panel of the RV she hadn't noticed before, secured the latch and then climbed back behind the wheel.

"Just checking to see that it was secure," he said in way of an explanation.

Weird.

It took another ten minutes to reach the speaker, and they placed their order. Another couple minutes and they were third in line, stomachs rumbling.

Mary watched as the pickup truck immediately in front of them pulled even with the window. A young woman working the register reached out, extending a food tray with a Tupperware-style bin secured on top, towards the driver. Nothing seemed to happen at first. The driver, it appeared to Mary, was slow in paying for their order.

Even over the rumblings of the Winnebago's less than stealthy engine, Mary and James could hear the pickup driver's words growing in volume.

Then the driver reached out and tossed a wad of crumpled bills into the bin, the employee dutifully pulling it back inside the restaurant.

"I wonder what that's about?" James asked for both of them.

Mary was silent, scrutinizing the scene that was unfolding in front of her, eyes narrowed and lips pursed, suspicion building.

When the bin reappeared again at the end of the young lady's arm, it hung there, momentarily ignored. More heated words could be heard before a large, beefy hand shot out and snatched the tray away from the young lady's grasp.

A few seconds later, Mary and James watched as the bin and tray assembly frisbeed out the passenger window of the truck, absent any cash, where it rattled around noisily on the pavement before coming to rest.

"Hold my beer," Mary said, dropping their code word that something was about to go down that shouldn't be missed. Before James could reach out and get a hold of his sister, Mary had taken off her seatbelt, dropped out of the vehicle, and was stomping towards the pickup up truck.

"Shit," he said, trying to open his own door, but the wall of the restaurant made the maneuver impossible to execute.

Mary bent over, picked up, and dusted off the bin and tray before turning to face the open passenger window of the pickup truck.

"Hey!" Mary yelled at the driver, startling both the irate man and the young lady. "What the hell is your problem?" she screamed.

He turned and glared at her, temporarily unable to fathom what exactly was happening.

"Why are you giving these employees a bunch of crap? They're being considerate and following company policy by using a tray and bin to retrieve payment and keep idiots like you safe!" she said, holding up the aforementioned bin and tray as evidence.

"How dare you?" the man spouted.

"How dare me?" she yelled back, ratcheting up the volume another notch. "People inside here are just trying doing their jobs, serving knuckleheads like you during a health emergency, and you have the gall to come here acting like a pompous jerk? Why do you think they deserve that? And why do you think you may act that way?" Mary demanded.

"I should get out of my truck and teach you some manners!" he threatened.

"Bring it! I dare you," she yelled back.

But like James a few seconds ago, the man couldn't get out through the driver's door. Realizing the logistical problem, the man punched the gas, and the truck shot thirty feet forward where it sat, brake lights blazing.

Mary's eyes remained fixed on the driver's mirrors, knowing he was looking back in her direction, a scary looking, teeth-bared woman, glaring in his direction.

"Bring it!" she yelled again, motioning for the man to back up his words with actions.

"Okay, that's enough. People are armed in this state," James said, finally reaching Mary's side.

James' appearance either presented two opponents now, or it deescalated the confrontation because the driver came off the brakes and the pickup pulled out into traffic and disappeared.

"That was close," James said.

Mary exhaled a chest full of air, all through her nose, already feeling the adrenaline fade.

"Betting against me?" she asked, slipping on her mask and walking towards the drive-thru window. The young lady's eyes were still wide in astonishment.

"Heck no," he answered.

Honks from behind prompted James to retrieve their ride and roll forward.

"Thank you for coming to work to serve your customers safely. I'm sorry you have to deal with people like that," she said, thumbing toward traffic. Mary handed the tray and bin back to the young girl, who looked both relieved and even younger, up close.

"He comes by here almost every day," she said. "Usually very pleasant."

"Well, you keep doing your job and keep up the good work, okay?" Mary asked.

The girl smiled and nodded. From behind her, a managerial type stepped up, setting a bag of food next to the window. "I'm afraid we can't serve you unless you're in a vehicle, ma'am. Regulations."

The manager himself couldn't have been over eighteen, Mary noted.

"You're absolutely right and good for you for enforcing it," she said, impressed.

She nodded, and took a half-dozen steps back from the window, allowed the RV to take her place.

Before she could climb back aboard, however, she felt another vehicle roll up behind her. Mary turned, ready for a fight if the driver of the pickup had made the unwise decision to circle back. She didn't need to worry, though, appreciating the scene in front of her. A shiny new SUV idled in front of her, the driver around her own age, appraising Mary from behind a pair of tinted shades. She didn't mind.

"Problem here?" he asked smoothly, just enough of an accent to remind her she was no longer in Michigan.

"No sir. No problems here," she said with a smile, almost at eye level with the rugged and tanned face of the Montana State Police officer behind the wheel. She found it difficult to maintain the six-foot, social distancing guideline, her body wanting to drift must closer.

Mary could see RV in her periphery swing into a parking spot off to the left, but never took her eyes or attention away from the uniformed officer.

The other cars in line continued to pull forward. Her brother had to be eating his lunch. And the screaming guy was probably halfway across the county by now. But to Mary, her entire world centered on this single conversation.

She brushed her hair back, tucking it behind an ear so she could get a better look at the man, her smile only widening beneath the mask.

The officer nodded, a smile on his own lips.

It was a beautiful smile, Mary noted, great teeth.

"Guy in the pickup truck acting irrational?" he asked, bringing the topic back around to the business at hand.

She nodded, admitting that he had been.

"Inconsiderate," she replied, trying to downplay the skirmish.

She always had a thing for guys in uniforms, she knew, still smiling under her mask, pissed that the trooper couldn't see it.

"Giving the crew a hard time?"

Again, she nodded, confirming his take on the events that had transpired.

"Yes," she admitted.

And he was not married, she couldn't help by notice, his left hand on the wheel, no hint of a ring in sight.

"Good for you," he replied. "Nutty times we're living in right now. All kinds of stress and anxiety."

She felt the flush of heat rush under the skin of her face at what she took to be a compliment.

"I know the man in the pickup truck. Normally a nice guy," he continued, watching her with his soft, brown eyes.

She nodded, wondering where all this was heading.

"That's what the young lady said," she added.

Mary was trying to focus on the officer's words, but her attention was more on how he said them, rather than what they meant.

"She doesn't know it," he said, nodding towards the woman working the drive-thru window, "but the man in the truck? He had to move his wife into hospice yesterday."

Shit.

"Do I need bail money?" her brother inquired, as Mary climbed back into the passenger seat. She yanked off her mask and shoved it into her pocket. She strapped in, took a deep breath, and without another word, reached down into the waxy, paper sack, searching for her cheeseburger.

"Or are you engaged?" James inquired. "I'm good either way. I just need to know if I should keep my Sundays open."

She nearly choked on her first bite.

"Just drive," she said, still reeling from what had transpired and her role in it, her righteous anger long evaporated. 'Judge not, lest ye be judged,' she remembered, chastising herself for jumping to conclusions. She should have known better. Mary had been a witness to someone being treated unfairly, and despite her better judgement, had leaped headlong into the fray. The pickup driver, regardless of his circumstances, had been wrong for lashing out like he had, but she could and should have handled it differently.

Probably a good thing that Jesus hadn't been here to see all that happen. If he was Him, she thought, then he saw it all go down, the sense of irony not escaping her.

30 – Murdo, South Dakota

"Might as well take a break and top off the tank," James commented. The incident at the lunch had provided only a momentary distraction from the guilt he was feeling at sending Jesus packing that morning. It hadn't been his best hour and now the churning in his guts was back and stronger than ever.

Pulling up to the pump, James switched off the engine. He moved to discard their trash, but he wasn't quick enough. Mary had bagged it all up, crushed the contents into an angry little ball, and tossed the mass out her window, missing the trash can entirely. She made no immediate move to climb out and remedy the situation, something she had never done before.

James' eye widened, waiting for Mary to climb down, but she just sat there staring blankly through the windshield.

"I'll get that," he said, as he backed out of the driver's door and shuffled around the front of the RV. Afraid to make eye contact as he walked by, he continued around back and started pumping gas, which the Winnebago seemed to burn in prodigious quantities.

After paying, he reluctantly returned to the driver's side door, but didn't immediately climb inside. Instead, he poked his face into the open window and found his sister still sitting there, seat belt on, arms crossed, a sneer present on her normally placid face.

"Want to drive?" he offered in a gentle and playful tone, holding up the keys.

Mary exhaled slowly, nostrils flaring, eyes never leaving the windshield.

"No. My head's not really in a good place right now," she rightfully admitted.

He nodded, clearly stalling.

"Want a slushie? Looked like they have them inside. I think I'm going to go back inside and get one."

Mary's nostrils flared again, the sounds of a long, slow intake of air reaching his ears.

"No, thank you."

"Okay. Anything else I can get you?"

Mary slowly shook her head, the movement almost imperceptible. He nodded and turned from the window, taking a slow stroll towards the building.

When he emerged a few minutes later, he climbed aboard and fired up the engine. Traffic was backed up on the only route out of the station's lot, so he headed into town, following the signs towards what he could only assume was a second route to the interstate. It took a moment before another driver, taking pity on the Winnebago, allowed it to inch out into the gap provided.

"Left at the intersection," Mary offered, looking at her phone. "Looks like our only option," she noted, trying her best to help their cause.

"Thanks."

They inched along, every other vehicle within miles headed in this same direction. When they finally made the turn minutes later, they were rewarded with another backup. Several people were out directing traffic. They could see emergency vehicles in the distance, lights flashing. Most of the cars and trucks ahead of them, including those in the oncoming lane, were turning off the road and disappearing from view behind the facades of several buildings that lined the street ahead.

As the town dwindled the further west they traveled, it wasn't an emergency that was snarling traffic. Some kind of event, clearly involving more people than the small town could have mustered, was about to get underway.

"Looks like a circus," James said.

"I think you might be literally correct," Mary replied, studying the scene in confusion. The upper reaches of a large, white, unadorned tent was just coming into view. Curiosity seemed to stir her out of the seething funk she had been harboring since lunch.

"Not exactly a wise thing to do," James tentatively offered.

Out her window, Mary could see people lining the grassy areas along the gravel shoulder, even the curbs and sidewalks from town having ended by this point. Folks were brandishing signs, while others were smiling and waving enthusiastically at the passing vehicles. James and Mary almost felt like rock stars, the Winnebago garnering more than its share of attention.

"It's like we've fallen in an alternate universe. Only a handful of these folks are wearing a mask and they're all walking shoulder to shoulder," she noted, watching the flow of foot traffic in the crosswalk ahead. Vehicular traffic stopped in both directions.

An elderly couple, strolling arm in arm, and the last two people to traverse the street, were both wearing masks, the only actual sign that the universe, in which the siblings now found themselves, was likely their own.

The woman looked up sheepishly at Mary, probably a bit embarrassed at their slow progress crossing in front of the RV and waved, thanking them for their patience. Mary could picture a tired smile on the woman's face as she helped the gentleman, cane in hand, with crossing the street.

That could likely be her in similar circumstances someday, so she smiled and waved back, acknowledging that things were fine, no harm done.

Not that they were going anywhere, she noted, the tail end of an SUV ahead of them having yet to fully clear the crosswalk itself.

"It's not a circus," she concluded, breaking the silence. "It's a church service."

Being fully stopped, with nowhere to go, James could sense the impending movement, but realized too late for him to do anything about it.

Mary, in one smooth motion that would have impressed even Houdini, had undone her seat belt, cracked her door, and slipped out the confines of the Winnebago before he could reach out and take hold of her. The door slammed and his sister drifted away, her mask in proper position.

He watched Mary as she jogged ahead and caught up to the elderly couple, maintaining a respectful distance. Even at their slow pace, they were making their way up the street faster than he was progressing in the RV.

Foot traffic was momentarily halted, and he finally had enough room in front to ease the RV past the pedestrian crossing.

The tent to his right, James noted, was set back off the road, behind several businesses. Most folks, including his sister and the elderly couple she was accompanying, found shortcuts between the businesses lining the road, and were quickly lost from sight.

Most of the traffic was turning onto a side street ahead and were queueing up to park. Beyond the flashing lights and people directing traffic at the corner, the road appeared wide open and beckoned.

"Dang it," James said, knowing he would have to wade the Winnebago deeper into the chaos in order to retrieve his sister. Mary's impetuous nature now had her somewhere in that mass of humanity. There would be little chance of him finding her in the crowd, so he elected to stay with the RV, its chunky white shape allowing it to stand out above most of the other vehicles.

After negotiating with a young man, who was waving a sad orange flag at passing vehicles, and passing him twenty bucks, James wiggled the RV into a spot that would allow him a reasonably simple escape when the time came.

James shut down the engine and had just gotten comfortable in the back for a nap when the side door opened and Mary appeared, snipping the bands and tossing her mask into the trash. She lathered a healthy dose of sanitizer onto her hands and rubbed it in thoroughly.

When James didn't immediately stir from his spot, Mary jumped up on the second bed, opposite the aisle from his and laid down.

"They're passing out masks to everyone going inside, so that's a good sign," Mary remarked, staring at the ceiling.

He studied her for a moment, but soon shook off the thought. Mary was no more likely to successfully rein in her impetuous nature as he was in loosening up his overly cautious side.

"Want to go back in? I don't mind waiting out here."

"What? No," she said, waving her hand as though giving it no serious consideration. "I still don't think it's a wise move, as you said, having this many people together in one place, masks or not. Many seemed to think that wearing it only over their mouth would be effective, while others, meeting the requirement, if not the intent, were wearing them more like a necklace."

"Seems to defy all logic."

"And the letter of the law, I suspect. But as we know from our own state, the laws only come into play if those charged with enforcing them actually choose to do their jobs," Mary noted, referencing several county sheriffs who had interpreted the law in a way they found convenient.

"Want me to drive, so you can rest?" she asked, noting that he had still made no move to get up.

"No. I didn't know how long you would be, so I was just killing time. Figured it would be easier for you to find the Winnebago than it would have been for me to find you."

They laid there in the silence, long enough for both of them to wonder if they'd find themselves still here come morning. Neither seem motivated to move forward, but neither seemed content to remain where they were.

Mary knew it was more mental than physical in her case, but what about her brother?

"If I gave you the option to turn the RV around and head home right now, would you take it?"

James considered the question for so long that she wondered if he had fallen asleep. Eventually, though, he looked over at her and answered. "No. We need to see this through."

Mary looked his way, considering his answer. "Could you continue on without me, then?"

As much as she tried, Mary couldn't keep from busting out laughing.

James smiled. "I knew you weren't serious, but I heard some truth in that question."

Mary grew quiet, considering his words. As though on cue, she could hear the hymnal music from the tent event penetrate the motorhome.

"I didn't know what to expect, but honestly, it wasn't this."

James chuckled this time, clearly in agreement.

"I didn't give it much thought. Dad always made these trips look so easy. But it's not the camper that's causing me pause, it's the circumstances."

"But you don't want to turn around and head home, do you?" she asked. "I could finish this. Dad and I could rent a motorcycle." she said.

It was a ludicrous idea that she would ever get on one of those contraptions, much less rent one, but the sentiment was real, and James didn't chuckle this time.

"I know you would, Mary, but we need to see this through as much for ourselves as for dad. Waiting a year or two for the pandemic to be over won't make this task any easier. And we've made it this far."

"We have," she conceded, a sense of pride building in her as the sounds of Amazing Grace grew in volume outside.

"We'll get you on my motorcycle once we get home," James said with mock seriousness, climbing to his feet.

31 – Wall, South Dakota

"I just don't get the appeal," Mary noted, staring at the large road sign that continued to grow the closer they got to the end of the exit ramp.

It was clear from the way she stated the question that Mary had no interest in visiting a museum right now, much less this one. James reached up, turned on the blinker, and committed the Winnebago to a left-hand turn instead of a right. She didn't object.

Cars and trucks and other RVs were evenly split, going in both directions from the stop sign, so it took a few moments before it was finally their turn to proceed.

"Explain it to me," Mary said, continuing her probe. She turned in her seat and stared at James, clarifying that she was still expecting an answer.

A break in traffic opened up, and he swung the Winnebago south, removing the only real reason he had for not answering. He shrugged, unsure what she wanted him to say. "I don't understand the question."

Mary looked amused now, scrunching up her mouth like his dodge left an unpleasant taste in it. He was clearly stalling.

"What is it with most men, probably American men, and their fascination with weapons," she asked, thumbing behind them, towards the museum that lay just beyond the exit in the opposite direction?

"I wouldn't say it's a fascination, per se," James defended meekly.

"Attraction? Obsession? Infatuation? Passion?" Mary offered. "Fetish, perhaps? Giant rockets with big payloads?"

she said, referring to the Minute-Man missile museum, two miles back.

James laughed, but it sounded tinged with unease. Mary was familiar with the sounds he made whenever she caught him in a similar, indefensible position.

"You really should have been on the debate team," he said, trying to compliment his way out of it.

"Stop stalling and answer the question."

This was usually the time when she, noting he wasn't going to bite, would give up, but Mary was bored and angry and she wasn't going to let this opportunity slip away.

"Do they make you feel powerful just by looking at them? Or do you have to fire them? Is it a sense of control? Do you feel you're in charge when carrying a firearm? Or is it about a lack of respect? Is it fear of others having them and not you? Is it a fear of losing them? Is it a competition? What is it exactly?"

Smartly resisting the urge, James decided that today was probably not a great day for him to push his luck.

"I need to stretch," he fibbed, pulling into the Badlands visitor center and hopping out. Mary had contemplated waiting in the RV but followed instead, slipping on her mask and making her way inside.

James went straight for the restrooms, but she, hands on her hips, silently evaluated the room and the other tourists inside. Information desk, pamphlets of local attractions, restrooms, dioramas, a small café, vending machines and the obligatory gift shop filled with the usual trinkets.

It wasn't a large building and the number of people inside was pretty high, social distancing not mathematically possible. The crowd was split 50/50 on mask wearing and applying hand sanitizer from the pedestal pumps set up on both sides of the entrance doors.

More folks were packed in here than she had seen in other parts of their trip, but this place was filled with cautious people visiting from other states, which had more stringent restrictions in place.

James emerged from the restroom and turned towards the café. Mary saw him point to the line, pantomiming a drinking motion. After a moment of indecision, she gave in, nodding. The turmoil continued roiling inside her, but she began to feel some relief, fatigue overcoming fight. She turned and stepped back outside, frustrated with both their lack of progress and because of it.

When James stepped outside, she was pacing around the RV like a caged animal, the tension palpable.

"Thanks," she muttered, taking her tea and returning to the shot-gun seat. She breathed deep, but the tea wasn't the one she hoped for. No reason it would be, she chided herself.

A mile down the road, an intersection appeared. James stopped, waited his turn, and then continued. Just when Mary had lost her enthusiasm for debate and had decided to quietly study the impressive badlands stretching out before them, she spoke again.

"Why did you just stop?"

James searched the rearview mirror, wondering if he had mistaken the sign at the intersection for something else. He was pretty sure he hadn't.

"Stop sign," he said, thumbing back out the driver's window.

"It's just a piece of red, painted metal."

He smiled and scrunched up his eyebrows in amused confusion.

"Because it's the law?" he reminded her.

"So, you stopped back there because it's the law?"

"Of course," he noted with a nervous chuckle. "What's up with you?"

If she had heard his question, she ignored it.

"So, if the law says you have to wear a mask in public, you do it right?"

"Well, probably, yes," he stammered, "If I thought the virus was as bad as they claim it is."

"Whether you follow the law depends on if you believe it's worth obeying?"

It finally dawned on him what she was doing. The defense attorney was back. Crap.

"You know. Stops signs, don't drink and drive, pay your taxes. That sort of thing," he defended.

"Sometimes, you're saying that the law is the law, but in others, it's a risk versus convenience decision?"

James huffed and wiggled uncomfortably in the driver's seat, finding it hard to sit still while under cross-examination. "It's not that simple," he said, trying to explain.

"Life's not black and white?"

She was baiting him now, but he didn't mind. This was good for her. Good for him too, in the long run.

"Yes, there are shades of gray in some areas," he had to admit.

"You're saying that in those gray areas, where people cannot see a value, laws are really more like guidelines?"

"Well, yes," he started. "And no," he finished.

At least Mary was smiling now, if in a 'gotcha' sort of way.

"I know you're talking about mask wearing and the declaration of an emergency in states like ours. People don't think the virus is that big of a threat," he started, holding up a hand to stay her objection. "In nursing homes, and for those with compromised immune systems, most people will admit that COVID-19 is potentially dangerous, even fatal."

She nodded, concurring. "So, even though the viral experts say it's dangerous and communicable and the emergency declaration says you have to wear a mask, people who think they're not at great risk, or will accept the risk should be able to ignore the mask requirement when they're out in public?"

Her brother's head wobbled back and forth, pondering his next words carefully.

"I see your point," he conceded. "But yes. Should someone like me, who isn't in the risk group, have to spend the money for masks and be inconvenienced wearing them?"

Mary nodded, as though evaluating his argument.

"What if you're actually a carrier and you're asymptomatic? You could spread the virus everywhere and not even know it. While someone else who is at risk then picks up the virus? Like if dad had to go to the store for groceries?"

Ouch. That last bit hurt, but he knew it wasn't a shot directed solely at him.

"Point taken."

"It's not about points, James. Everyone who catches this bug picked it from someone else."

Another point taken, but he didn't voice it this time.

"With Michigan, if the governor had simply notified people of the risks, I'm confident that they would have done the right things, like wearing their masks or keeping their distance."

Mary laughed now, in a deep-seated, funniest-thing-you've-ever-said sort of way.

"Are you listening to yourself?" she asked, and although it had come out harshly, she didn't seem apologetic.

"That's the rationale I've heard anyway," he defended, watering down his own argument.

"By people who don't wear masks, don't social distance, and advocate keeping society completely open?"

"Yes," he had to admit.

"Do you honestly think that everyone, if instructed to close their shops, stay home, keep their distance, and wear a mask in public, would have voluntarily complied if the governor had simply encouraged it? They aren't doing it now and it's the law!"

When she put it that way, his belief didn't really hold water.

"I think most would," he said.

Mary shook her head in disbelief at both the sentiment and her brother's faith in society. Before the pandemic, she might have agreed, but now? The cynicism she harbored was picking away at her. If you couldn't believe that your neighbors had the best interest of society at heart, what did you really have?

"The governor says you need to close your businesses temporarily and stay home. You're claiming that most people would have complied?"

"Yes," James stated with a lack of conviction.

"People who are living day by day, paycheck to paycheck, would voluntarily shut down and not be able to pay their rent or buy groceries?"

"Yes," he said again, even less confident this time.

"And those who say they won't. They get to keep working, earning a living, paying their bills, not racking up debt, and taking on new customers, who have left the places where they currently shop, because their suppliers have done the right thing and shut down until given the all clear?"

"Maybe."

"No one is going to do that, James. They have fought too long to win their customers and clients. None of them would give all that up voluntarily and start over while their competitors were going to stay open. Our convictions and memories are way too short."

Mary heard the tone in her words and the sound disgusted her. How far she had fallen, she realized, with a sinking feeling.

James signaled and pulled off onto a gravel turnout, catching Mary off guard. They had come all this way to see the badlands, but their conversation had hijacked their attention and they had already missed most of it.

"Despite always being on the defensive with you, Mary, I wouldn't trade our conversations for anything, but we can't leave here without at least taking glance at this hole in the ground."

32 – Rapid City, South Dakota

"Want ice cream? I think we need ice cream," James declared, swinging the RV over into the turn lane before Mary could object.

With no drive-thru at this old-fashioned ice cream parlor, it meant that they had to go inside. The hostess approached, and after noting their masks, visibly frowned as though it were a reflection on the cleanliness of both her and her place of employment. A few groups at tables nearby also took note. Looks of displeasure spread across their sticky faces. With arms crossed, the hostess' body language spoke volumes. For several uncomfortable seconds, it was silent until Mary attempted to break the deadlock.

"Just the two of us," she confirmed flatly.

A few seconds later, the young woman caved, grabbing two menus and turning. She didn't bother instructing them to follow, but they did so anyway. It appeared, as they passed through the sea of occupied tables, that they were headed for the back, which suited Mary fine, as it was far less crowded.

"You know, we don't have that here," the hostess informed them.

Mary and James had to remain standing, unable to deduce which table was theirs.

"And if we did," she continued. "That virus isn't any more harmful than the regular flu."

Mary congratulated herself for reigning in a nearly unquenchable desire to roll her eyes. With her irritable mood fully entrenched, she knew that now wasn't the time to delve into the statistical nuances of fatalistic curves relating to the current pandemic.

"That's what I thought too," James said, moving towards her for a fist bump. For his efforts, the woman rewarded him by taking a few steps back and holding up a hand, signaling a different message.

"Whoa. Six feet buddy," she declared.

With his eyebrows knitted together in confusion, he held his advance.

"I thought you said there was nothing to worry about?" James asked.

"There's not, but you're creeping me out and the whole social distancing thing is a convenient way for me to keep you at a comfortable distance." Having determined that her obligation to them was at an end, she dropped the menus on the nearest table and retreated.

"That was weird," he admitted, once the young woman was out of earshot. Everyone else had already gone back to their own meals and conversation, the novelty of the new arrivals forgotten.

Mary made a noise that might have been agreement, her eyes scanning the offerings.

"You were quiet," James noted.

"I try not to antagonize people that have access to food or drink that I'm about to consume," she said. "No matter how much I might want to."

"Wise advice."

"Thanks. Great idea, stopping by the way."

"Welcome. I thought so too."

Their server approached, another young woman about the same age as the hostess. This employee, though, was wearing a mask.

"Get any grief?" she asked, stepping up to their table.

Mary nodded, keeping any commentary to herself.

"Sorry about that. Owner's daughter. Doesn't have any apprehension in letting others know what she thinks about everything."

Mary nodded again. "Do you get any grief?"

"I've worked here for years now and am more or less invisible to her. Comments on my mask happened for the first few days, but then she ran out of witty things to say."

Mary had to give her credit; their server didn't seem at all flustered by the situation.

"Has to be rough."

"Only if you let it," the woman conceded. "I keep coming back, so it can't be that bad."

"Worried about the virus?" James asked.

"Not really, although no healthy person knows for sure if they're susceptible, from what I've been reading in the journals. Even something as simple as a blood type could alter your chances of a getting a more severe case or having more severe complications."

"Pre-med?" Mary inquired, noting that the young woman hadn't mentioned the news. She guessed that anyone delving into that kind of detail was either into social issues, like her, or was likely in the medical profession.

"Nursing degree over here at USD," she said, thumbing over her shoulder towards the north. "But pre-med is on my roadmap."

"Good for you," Mary said, and she meant it.

"Thank you. Decide what you'd like to eat?"

After splitting a chili cheese fry, they finished their ice cream, paid their bill, left a generous tip, and then slipped out while the hostess had temporarily abandoned her post.

33 – Keystone, South Dakota

They dropped off the interstate and onto a thin ribbon of asphalt labeled as US-16. They passed all kinds of touristy stops trying to attract visitors that either had time to kill or had a sense of obligation. None were open, but it wouldn't have mattered. Mary and James were focused now, cognizant of the late afternoon hour.

They were both surprised to find that visiting Mt. Rushmore didn't cost a dime to get in, but you had to pay to park. Thankfully, the lines were short, and they were quickly allowed through.

Along the roadway, temporary signs explained that although the destination was open for viewing, the facilities were not open for use and that they should plan accordingly.

They rode in their temporary home and thankfully; it had all the normal conveniences to which they were accustomed.

"Maybe we could charge for the use of our bathroom?" James offered, to offset some of their costs. From the look that Mary shot him, however, it probably wasn't an approval for his plan.

They parked, got out, were detoured around the expansive gift shop and directed down a short trail to a large, marble-lined viewing area. Ahead and below, an outdoor seating area where guides would normally give their historic pitch to throngs of tourists was taped off. There would be no talks given today.

With tours canceled and buildings locked up, only the occasional employee could be seen scurrying about. Probably maintenance employees, Mary pondered, as the two of them had the entire viewing area to themselves.

Both he and Mary took out their phones, got a few shots of the monument and took a selfie together as there was no one immediately around to assist them. They didn't want to hand off their phones anyway; they decided.

Mary then returned her phone to her pocket and tried to take in the scene. She had been far too preoccupied on other trips, with taking the perfect photo, that she never truly stopped to enjoy the locale while she was still there. She was working to change that though by trying to be fully present.

"I figured it would be larger," James said, staring up at the four busts of former presidents.

"Me too, but we are over a quarter of a mile away. Can recognize the portraits anyway."

"Very true."

"The trail is open to get a closer look. Interested?"

James surveyed the route, most of it hidden in the tree-line and noting the climb out that would be required, passed. "I'll just meet you at the camper."

"Sure thing. Probably a half hour. I'll call you if I find something cool or it takes longer."

"Sounds good."

Mary followed the signs that lead off of the viewing platform to her left and joined a trickle of folks making their way downhill towards the base of the mountain, while James found little to check out, with the building locked up tight. Having time to kill, he meandered back towards the Winnebago, studying the various plaques posted in the garden along the winding walkway.

It only took minutes before he had traversed the acre sized area twice and got bored. He was checking his phone for messages when he stepped back into the parking lot and paused, a disconcerting feeling washing over him. Not more than fifty feet ahead, the door to a Winnebago was open and a figure, framed by the opening, was watching him. James looked up, confused. His eyes moved to the left, then to the right, and then back to the young man standing in the doorway. There were no other vehicles nearby that were similar enough to their RV to be mistaken.

The young man, still on the steps, arms full of stuff, looked surprised at first, clearly not expecting his return so soon. Then he looked a bit freaked out. Finally, his eyes sparkled, and a smirk passed across his lips. Before James could move, the kid was down on the concrete, his running shoes getting solid traction.

"Damn it. Stop!" James yelled after him, while in pursuit. He had run track in high school, but that had been a lifetime ago, and he hadn't exactly been preparing for this eventuality.

But the adrenaline was flowing and having seen what the thief had stolen provided plenty of motivation.

"Mary is going to kill me," he mumbled under his breath, somewhat encouraged that the distance between the two of them was closing.

The young man, apparently surprised by a quick look over his shoulder, dug deeper and could maintain the gap.

"Where do you think you're going?" James yelled out. If he rattled the kid, it didn't show. It only encouraged him to move faster. Finding a break in the parked cars, the thief ducked to his right and was lost from James' view for a few moments. An SUV, swinging into that coveted spot required James to detour wide, costing him critical seconds.

"Where is he?" James asked himself, tiring from the sprint. He continued moving forward as fast as possible, but had lost sight of his target.

As he began a systematic search under each vehicle, the rumble of a heavy diesel engine drew his attention. Not recognizing either man in the pickup truck, he was preparing to write it off, when a familiar face sat up in the bed and looked his way. The young man nodded to James as though congratulating him on a good, but unsuccessful race, and then threw him a half-hearted salute, his ride speeding up, headed for the exit.

James stood there dumbfounded, more sweat pouring off his face than the sprint should have generated. He felt sick. Like, really, really bad. What was he going to do now? If the thief had made off with a few small things, no loss, but their father's ashes? He could clearly picture the stained wooden box in the young man's arms. No way that could be replaced. Mission over.

"The Winnebago!" James shouted, realizing that a chase in the humble RV was the only course of action left open to him, albeit a weak one. He spun, keys in hand, prepared to set a new personal record for his sprint back to the camper, when he froze, eyes wide.

Standing off to one side, unnoticed until a moment ago, stood Jesus. Cradled in his arms was a familiar-looking box, folded flag resting respectfully on top.

Jesus smiled, face beaming.

Time was ticking away. James was afraid that this was some kind of crazy hallucination spawned from the guilt he still held on to.

"What's happening?" James sputtered; his brain unable to piece together the seemingly unconnected facts into any kind of rational picture.

He stepped towards Jesus, hesitant to get too close, afraid that the man was only a delirious illusion. By now, he knew, the pickup truck would be long gone, his window for pursuit, closed. All of his eggs were in this unlikely and unassuming basket, standing not more than five feet in front of him.

"I told him he couldn't have these," Jesus explained, holding out the items to James.

James reached out slowly, just touching the polished box at first to confirm it was real. Then he took it in his hands and squeezed it firmly, the solidity causing waves of relief to course through his weary limbs. Several uncontrollable sobs followed a nervous chuckle, each shaking him to the core. Losing these remains would have devastated Mary and might have killed him.

"I don't understand," James cried, shaking his head back and forth in confusion.

Instead of answering, Jesus turned like he was making to leave, and stepped away.

"Wait!" James blurted out, tears pouring down his face. "You can't leave!"

Jesus turned back and smiled.

"Technically, you *could* leave," James clarified. "But please don't go. I was wrong before." He felt his knees weaken, unsure if it meant his legs were about to give out, or that he should be kneeling.

Jesus nodded, as though agreeing to stay, walking back together towards the RV. James would have hugged the man if his arms hadn't been full, but there was no way he was setting down the box.

"When we see Mary though," he said, sniffing back tears, "could we keep what happened before and here, just between us, you know, man to man?" he asked.

Before Jesus could answer, they rounded the Winnebago and found Mary standing there, examining the side door of the RV.

"Jesus!" she practically screamed, racing over and grabbing him in a bear hug, like the man at the gas station had done. She could now relate to what the man had been experiencing.

Mary smiled at her brother, then looked perplexed when she saw the items he was carrying.

"Why do you have dad's ashes?" she asked.

"Look who I found!" James said, nodding his head towards Jesus. When she wouldn't bite, he gave in. "Took him for a walk?"

"Flag too?" she asked, brows furrowed.

"Sure," James added, clearly not selling the narrative.

Jesus stepped forward, and it seemed to break the spell. Mary hugged him again, and the tears resumed. She tried to put into words the flood of emotions welling up inside her, but nothing recognizable came out.

"I'm glad to see you too," he said, letting her off the hook.

"Where did you go?" she sputtered. "Why did you leave?"

James froze, wondering how this was going to go down.

"I had to find a solitary place to pray," Jesus said, not answering the question, but not totally ignoring it, either.

"Just like Mark and Luke wrote, right? That's cool." James said, climbing aboard and securing dad in his spot. "We should probably get going. Everyone ready to go? I'm ready to go. We should go."

"What's the matter with the door?" she asked.

James dropped to the ground and let Jesus climb in the back. He then opened the passenger door for his sister and she got in.

"It's old, sis. I'm sure it just needs a little TLC. I'll take care of it, don't worry."

He closed Mary's door and then slammed the side door to the Winnebago a few times before leaning all his weight against it. He thought he felt the latch catch and let go. It seemed secure, mostly, so he backed away and jogged around to the driver's side.

James belted in, took and expelled a deep breath, and closed his eyes for a moment, trying to shake off all the craziness he had collected over the past hour.

"Ready to go, Jesus?"

Jesus nodded.

"You ready to go, sis?"

Mary nodded.

"How was your walk?" James asked, as he swing the Winnebago out of the lot.

34 – Custer, South Dakota

They had known the park was closed, but had hoped to have a decent view of the monument, even from the overnight parking lot where they would spend the night. The Winnebago pulled off at the entrance to the Crazy Horse Mountain site, and they were relieved to find that ample parking was indeed still available.

There was something poetic, Mary thought, that they had selected Custer, South Dakota, as the construction site for the monument to the former Lakota leader, Crazy Horse. Certainly, couldn't be a coincidence, could it? Mary pondered.

"It wasn't a good time for his people," Jesus commented as they got out to stretch.

Mary was disappointed at how far away the monument stood.

A converted tour bus was parked next to them, an older, African American couple seated comfortably under their awning. It might have provided shade for them an hour ago, but the setting sun was already dropping quickly towards the horizon.

The pair had masks around their necks but weren't wearing them at the moment as they relaxed and drank from well-used, Auburn school mugs. Mary waved in greeting and the two acknowledged with gentile nods.

Facing their new neighbors and racing against the sunset, the trio quickly set up their small grill and folding chairs.

"You don't mind if we grill, do you?" Mary asked, realizing that the masks could have been for medical reasons other than the virus.

"Oh no, help yourselves. We just got done, but thank you for asking," the woman answering for both of them with an accent Mary couldn't hope to place. The collegiate gear from the university in Alabama might have been a clue, but as Mary had painfully learned earlier, there were risks involved in making assumptions.

James fired up the BBQ and tossed on the burgers. Mary brought out the fixings and laid everything out on the small table she had unpacked.

Jesus emerged with plastic mugs and a matching pitcher, an unknown substance sloshing around inside. They each pulled down their masks and took a sip of what had looked like Kool-aide, but was actually the most delicious of chilled, red wine, a hint of fresh fruit.

When he motioned to their neighbors, they accepted the offer, draining their current drinks from the mugs in front of them. He filled them up and then returned to his own side, pulling down the mask and taking a long sip of his own, testing the concoction as he settled into his chair.

"Did you pick up more wine?" James turned and whispered to his sister.

She shook her head, a clear 'no'. Only drinks inside were James' remaining beers and a few diet pops.

"Delicious," the neighbors complimented.

"I've become a fan of sangria lately. Didn't have oranges growing up. I hope you don't mind the addition."

"Oh no, it fabulous," Mary said, clearly meaning it. She wondered if this was another miraculous Jesus event that they were witnessing, their neighbors unaware of the potential implications of what they were drinking. Like so many people, a miracle could happen and the couple across from them wouldn't be the wiser.

Mary was equally guilty, she realized, a slight downer on her mood until she looked up and saw Jesus studying her. Although she had witnessed the pain on his face back in Sioux City, she couldn't help but feel full hope now.

As James handed out the burgers, Mary opened the pleasantries.

"What are you all thinking about all the pandemic?" she floated, hoping to get a feel for where they stood.

"It could still turn into a real mess," the woman replied. She explained she was a retired doctor with a compromised immune system. "That's why we came out west; to get out of the big city. It was a risk, but with common sense and caution, we'll get through it."

"How about what they're doing in Sweden?" James asked. He hadn't said it with the usual confrontational tone that Mary was familiar with, but in a way that seemed genuine.

The woman's eyes flashed first to Mary, saw the 'look', and then returned to James, saying that in a pandemic like this, there is a cost to be paid, no matter the actions taken.

"In dollars or in lives, the bill is going to come due. But if we let data lead, there are many decisions we can make that will lessen the impact of both. With each poor decision, the tab goes up. The higher it goes, however, as we use up our supplies, burn out our hospital employees, and overwhelm our medical resources, the faster that tab increases." The woman looked again at Mary to see how she did.

'Thank you.' Mary mouthed, much to the woman's amusement. Unseen by anyone else, the woman nodded subtly to her left, at her husband, who seemed oblivious to the gesture, communicating that both her husband and James, seemingly, were cut from the same cloth when it came to their beliefs on the virus.

"Hadn't the virus already evolved by the time it reached the now famous market? Adapted for us as a host?" Mary prompted, guessing that although the woman was retired, she was probably still intrigued by it all.

The woman had clearly considered this angle and had given it some thought. "Some of my associates and I have talked about it at length and I think you're right. It seemed highly adapted to our physiology when those first people at the market came down with it."

"Could it have escaped from a lab? I heard there is a pretty big one in Wuhan," James questioned, apparently trusting in an authoritative source other than his sister. But she didn't mind the question and was eager to hear what the doctor had to say.

"There is a facility there and while I can't discount the potential that samples of it might have been in the lab prior to the market exposure, I don't think it was weaponized, engineered, or altered. If it was there, it was likely contained in a blood draw of someone sick in the area and they didn't know what they had."

"But because of the adaptation, you don't think it jumped from animals to humans?" Mary prompted, clearly intrigued and wanting a clarification.

"Because it was so well adapted to humans, as you noted, it's my guess that it probably jumped from animals to humans in the region, and then got passed around a closed community for a while before a carrier, not likely realizing they were still sick or were even asymptomatic, visited the market. Eventually, it got out of Wuhan before they could, or were unwilling, to contain it there. I would think it was the prior. No government, with a population the size of China, would want something like this to reach their other large population centers. Total chaos would ensue, as we're seeing now."

Mary was grateful to have what she thought was a sane voice around her. Then again, she remembered, people often felt sources were credible if they agreed with their own perceptions, herself included. It was a bias that was very hard to overcome and a trap that was easy to fall into.

"But wouldn't it have hit Beijing first, after Wuhan?" James countered.

"In the past, probably. But Wuhan has a population now of over ten-million people, barely keeping it in the top-ten in China. It's a major hub for manufacturing companies from across the globe and has its own international airport, so folks don't need to travel through other cities in China in order to get out of the country. The speed with which we can cross the globe is now our biggest Achilles' heel. Almost as much as our reliance on electricity, running water, sanitation, and the Internet."

The sun was obscured now as a line of clouds approached from over the western horizon. With the source of heat gone for the day, temperatures began dropping. More vehicles pulled in, the evening breeze kicking up dust as they jockeyed for a parking spot.

Having finished eating, and trying to wave away the dust with her hands and having no effect, she remembered her mask and slipped it back on, James doing the same.

"Aren't you uncomfortable?" she asked Jesus, who seemed unphased.

"It's actually kind of soothing. I grew up with it, getting into everything. Couldn't eat a meal without it being dusty. Learned to treat it like a spice," he said, laughing.

"You all have a great night," the woman said, as they headed inside for the night.

"You too," Mary said.

35 – Newcastle, Wyoming

The rolling and swaying of US-16 made US-20, on which they had spent so much time, look like a major freeway. Even the sign welcoming them to Wyoming was a modest affair. As each state passed behind them, Mary could feel her apprehension grow. With only a small stretch of 'The Equality State' laying between the Winnebago and Montana, her anxiety deepened.

Mary knew it was happening, having caught herself laying off the gas a few times, trying to delay the inevitable. James had pointed it out so many times, in fact, that Mary felt obliged to set the cruise control to ensure they kept moving forward.

When James headed to the back for a morning siesta, Jesus took up the shotgun seat and kept Mary company.

"I'm so glad you came back," she reiterated, for what seemed like the umpteenth time.

"I'm glad to be back," Jesus replied.

"I have so many questions and feared I wouldn't have time to ask them. And I'm still not sure exactly where we're headed or what I'm doing," she said, her voice trailing off.

"You're doing great, Mary. You just need to have a bit more faith in yourself."

It was hard to not smile with a compliment like that. She didn't believe it, but it was good to have something to shoot for. "Thank you."

"You're welcome. What questions?"

Mary paused, suddenly finding herself overwhelmed with inquiries, yet unable to pull one up that seemed appropriate. She could see that Jesus was giving her his undivided attention. He had a way of doing that. She was also relieved she had to keep her eyes on the road instead of trying to hold his gaze. Finally, she latched onto a topic that had been nagging her.

"The pandemic. Why?" she sputtered, unable to fully put her thoughts into words.

"Why did the Father unleash the pandemic on the world?"

Mary shook her head. "No, I don't think he did that based on what you said before." At least she hoped that the vengeful God that so many Christians seemed to worship wasn't the one ruling the universe.

"He didn't, Mary. That's not in His nature," Jesus assured her.

"But He is allowing it to happen though, right?"

Jesus studied Mary for a moment, seeing the pain and doubt in her sad eyes.

"He always has a plan, and it is for the greater good. You know that, right?"

She nodded, relieved, as if confused. "What possible good could come out of all this?"

"Maybe your brother, while out at lunch, was going to run into his ex-wife and it would have been detrimental to both of their lives? The airlines, bringing his ex-wife home from meetings in Europe, got canceled, and she made it onto another flight just before it left. But the Father couldn't allow that flight to be canceled because a doctor, traveling on that same plane, who will eventually lead the world towards a cure for cancer, had a funding meeting scheduled that he couldn't miss. And after the flight landed, your former sister-in-law had a craving for a steak and cheese sub. A flat tire might have stopped her unplanned rendezvous, but it would have meant that the gentleman on call from the roadside assistance company, would have been sent out to deal with it, and his very pregnant wife, about to give birth early, would have been left home alone. So, before your brother's ex-wife could get to the restaurant, and because of the pandemic and shelter-in-place orders, the owner sent everyone home early and locked up, preventing James and his ex-wife from crossing paths again and rekindling an old flame."

Mary's eyes widened, her mouth hanging open.

"You're telling me that the entire, global pandemic, that has shut down lives everywhere, was allowed to happen by God, just so my brother wouldn't run into, and rekindle his relationship with his ex-wife?!" she asked, trying to stifle a bout of hysterical laughter.

Her eyes studied the rearview mirror, hoping James hadn't heard any of this. He already had a very well-developed sense of self-importance, and this would have made him impossible to be around.

"Well, after thousands of years and billions of human interactions, sometimes extreme measures are needed to make sure all of the Father's plans come to fruition."

Mary was clearly struggling to keep up with the enormity of the revelation.

"Or none of that was true," Jesus said, laughing.

She took a quick glance his way and could see that he was joking about all of it.

"None of it?" she asked.

"Nope. I just wanted to let you know the Father loves each of you so much that He *would* go to great lengths for each one of you."

"So, this isn't about my brother at all?" she asked, wanting confirmation. She felt like smacking him in the arm for yanking her chain, but it felt sacrilegious. Jesus, though, was leaning against his door, laughing, staying just out of reach in case Mary changed her mind. She was smiling too, so he didn't feel overly threatened.

"The pandemic wasn't solely about James," Jesus admitted. "So many are being affected, in so many ways, that only our Father could ever hope to manage all the ramifications. Travel plans canceled, human interactions delayed, people passing from this world into the next in order to prevent prolonged suffering. Babies brought into the world that wouldn't have been conceived otherwise. We can't ever hope to fully grasp it all."

The topic was weighing on her heart and Mary doubted if asking such questions was a wise choice on her part. But she also couldn't afford to let such a rare opportunity pass, if Jesus was truly the one. Mary was still conflicted.

Questions and answers flowed back and forth, Jesus asking almost as many as Mary. Then she exhaled loudly, confident that Jesus had to have heard it, but if he did, he didn't comment. In the distance, she spotted a small sign which signified that they were passing into Wyoming, 'The Equal Rights' state.

It took another ten miles before signs of civilization began to appear on the horizon.

"Ready for breakfast?" Mary asked.

"Always," Jesus replied.

Mary, Jesus, and a still groggy but famished James, staggered into the diner.

Half the tables were occupied and nearly all of them, once the trio stepped inside, had turned to look in their direction. Not a single person, save for the three of them, was wearing masks. Mary assumed, by the novelty of their appearance, that few in this small town were likely following the CDC guidelines. She knew Jesus was fine with being observed and that James was probably unaware that people were staring at them, but she was feeling self-conscious under the gaze of the locals. Hopefully, they wouldn't catch any grief over their choice of face coverings from the staff.

"Three for breakfast? Or are you here to perform surgery?" the server inquired.

The woman had delivered it in such a deadpan way, not a hint of humor on her face, that Mary couldn't help but grin, grateful that the mask was hiding her reaction.

A loud cackling noise emanated from the kitchen, a sun-beaten and wrinkled face, hairnet pulled across a balding crown of a scalp, appeared in the window above a set of plates loaded with food.

"Hope they aren't here for me; I ain't got no insurance," the man said, before he disappeared from view, a deep, reverberating cough echoing from beyond.

"Just breakfast then, I guess," James answered, in an equally deadpan manner, looking towards the kitchen in horror. The woman appeared to lack a sense of humor, as she shrugged, grabbed three menus and led them to a table near the back. The patrons that were already seated nearby tried without success to look disinterested, as the trio followed her over and sat down. Mary felt like keeping her mask on, but took it off after they ordered. There were furtive glances in their direction and she couldn't help but feel as though they were evaluating her appearance. 'Maybe she's disfigured, and that's why she's wearing it?' she imagined them whispering to each other in hushed tones.

Once they had all determined that she was not horribly disfigured, the diners seemed to lose interest and the trio was soon, blissfully, forgotten.

The server, adorned in a diner-style uniform, returned with an armful of plates. She held up the first one and then called out the contents, despite knowing it was clearly James' breakfast.

"Organic, egg-white, spinach, sausage and cheese omelet, hold the sausage and cheese, with a double order of avocado and wheat toast, not toasted?"

James tried to motion that it was his, without alerting the entire restaurant, but she wasn't going to let him off that easily.

"Mine," he confirmed, in a loud tone that matched hers. He waited until the other diners turned back to their own meals before taking off and pocketing his mask.

She and Jesus had been prepared and had ordered exactly as the menu dictated, so they were spared the ordeal of acknowledging their order and it was set, correctly, if not gently, in front of each of them.

"Thank you," Jesus said simply, and the woman nodded, a hint of a smile on her lips.

"Need anything else?" she asked.

"No, thank you," he said, looking up at her. "It looks wonderful."

Satisfied, she moved off and checked on her other customers.

"Completely distinct feeling here, isn't it?" James asked, once their nearest neighbors had paid their bill and left.

"Almost like the virus doesn't even exist," Mary said, wondering if anyone in this town had contracted the virus or might succumb to its impact.

When Jesus turned her way and opened his mouth to speak, Mary stopped him.

"I don't want to know," she decided, waving him off.

He closed his mouth, nodded, and then turned his attention back to his perfectly prepared hash browns.

When they had finished up and stepped back outside, a thought occurred to Mary.

"Did you want to drive, Jesus?" she asked.

"Me? Oh no. I tried that once, and it didn't go well," he replied, seemingly happy to ride in the back and stare out the window. "Unless you need me to, or want me to. I could give it another try."

"No, we're good," James said, answering for them both.

36 – Moorcroft, Wyoming

"Wait, let me see if I'm following you. You're telling me that two atoms, if entangled, and taken to the opposite ends of the universe, will still know the quantum state of the other, instantly, even if separated by billions of light-years?" Mary said.

"Crazy, isn't it? The Father came up with quantum mechanics and hard-wired it into the design of the universe just to keep things interesting."

"But did He actually plan out where every single molecule would end up?" she asked.

"Didn't need to. He came up with a set of laws to govern it all. The four fundamental forces you know about, conversion of matter to energy and back again, wavelengths of energy, time and space, etcetera. He then spoke into being everything that will ever be and then let the laws do their thing. He's always dabbling, of course, to fine tune things here and there, but he put most of it in motion and simply let it go."

Mary was stunned at the revelations, her brain trying to grasp the enormity of it all as Jesus continued.

"Don't get me wrong, He's had a hand in it all, but mostly at a high level. The rest, again based on His laws, work out the details on their own. Except where humans are involved. He takes great interest and pride in his most treasured creations."

"And he's everywhere, always?" she asked.

"Oh yes," Jesus said. "Time has no bearing where He's concerned."

"But the universe is so large. How is that possible, even for God?"

"Remember entanglement? Clever humans are only now figuring out how to entangle atoms, but all the matter and energy in the universe is entangled. Humans just haven't discovered how yet."

"Like the force from *Star Wars*?" she asked.

He laughed at the simplified example. "Basically, yes."

"So, you're telling me that God invented quantum mechanics, wove it into everything, and because everything in the universe is entangled, it allows God to know the state of everything, everywhere, always?" Mary confirmed, dumbfounded.

"It's a lot more technical, of course, but you've got the general idea. Mind blown yet?" Jesus asked.

That was an understatement, she thought.

"Does that mean a highly localized God knows everything going on everywhere, or is He everywhere, knowing what's happening at every location in the universe?"

"Both!" Jesus replied, laughing, clearly enjoying himself. "And all the animals are hard-wired to behave a certain way, what you would call instinct. But not humans. In order for you to have free-will, you have brains that use quantum mechanics."

"You're kidding?"

"Nope, I kid you not. You couldn't have free-will without it. And as humans who have free-will, your brains can entertain several options when given a choice. And all the probabilities of all those options remain as possibilities, not collapsing into a single outcome, until you commit to a specific action."

"Whoa. I'm not sure what to think anymore."

"Crazy stuff." Jesus had to admit.

"OK. If God designed the rules relevant to how the universe operates, does that mean those rules apply equally everywhere?

"Yes, except in black holes, remember?"

"And instead of micromanaging everything, God set the rules for how the universe would operate, started its birth, and then let it basically unfold on its own?"

"No need to mess with it. It came into being exactly as He envisioned it would," Jesus said.

"Okay. But with a universe this big and all of us trapped on this single, little planet, does that mean that God has created life elsewhere or has plans to?"

"Carl Sagan said, 'If it's just us, it seems like an awful waste of space,'" Jesus replied.

"So did Jodie Foster's character in the movie *Contact*! I love that movie."

"Me too," Jesus acknowledged.

"So, what's the answer, then?" Mary pushed, clearly wanting to hear the answer.

Jesus leaned forward, the answer to her question on the tip of his tongue.

"I didn't understand that movie at all," James interrupted, staggering his way up to the front of the RV.

"What didn't you get?" she wondered.

"We better stop for gas, sis," James noted, before he could answer. "If the gas gauge has been there a while, we might run on fumes. Don't think the needle ever goes below a quarter of a tank."

"Not sure. I haven't been keeping track," she admitted, signaling as the next exit appeared on the horizon.

37 – Gillette, Wyoming

"Do you know where you'll be spending eternity?" the booming voice called out. "Because you'll be finding out soon! Jesus is on his way!"

"He's already here and closer than you think," James replied, as he and Mary dodged around the man and scooted past on the sidewalk

"Amen brother!" he said, not catching the double-meaning in James' comment.

"We need to get a window seat for this show," he said, holding the door open for his sister, who didn't reply, nor objecting.

"Booth by the window work?" The server asked, grabbing some menus.

"Yes please. There's three of us," Mary noted.

They slid into the booth and looked out, seeing Jesus break away from his conversation with a young couple on the far sidewalk and begin making his way towards them.

Instead of stepping around the man, Jesus stepped up and spoke a few words. Jesus still had his mask on, so they didn't stand a chance of even reading his lips.

The man began the conversation with a wide smile, speaking and then listening. Then his disposition changed, but the smile never left his face. His mouth opened, his eyes widened, and lines of tears spilled down his cheeks. Jesus reached up a hand and placed it on the man's shoulder for a moment as he nodded enthusiastically. When Jesus finally turned to come inside, the man, overwhelmed by emotion, had sunk to his knees and was smiling skyward, his homemade sign slipping from his fingers to the sidewalk.

Jesus stepped inside, bowed slightly to the server as he entered, and joined his friends in their booth.

While Jesus scanned the menu, James and Mary continued to watch the scene unfolding outside. The man, finally gaining some composure, used the rough, brown sleeve of his robes to wipe away the tears and stand, snatching up his sign and stuffing it into the trash bin next to him. He looked over at them, a face beaming with emotion, and nodded before turning and walking away.

James was shaken. When he turned his gaze upon his sister, Mary was watching him with a single raised eyebrow and a look of satisfaction on her lips.

"Ready to order?" The young man asked.

The restaurant was nearly empty, so the bored kitchen staff kicked out their order in record time.

Mary asked Jesus to say grace, and his eloquent words were, once again, inspiring.

"Amen," Mary said. "That was exquisite, Jesus. Thank you."

"It was," James added with uncharacteristic zeal.

They dug in and were silent for a moment, each savoring their food.

"You're going to turn into a burger," James noted, as Mary savored the beef patty.

She shrugged and mumbled something under her breath that sounded like 'Bright knee'.

James chuckled, giddy. Jesus was smiling. The playful banter between the siblings was a good sign that the pain at losing their father had subsided for a time, healing having already begun.

"I don't know if you've been getting antsy, sis," James began, a heaviness settling in again. "But we're getting close to the border and have to decide on which way to go."

She took another big bite, trying to buy herself a few moments to face up to the situation that she had been putting off for far too long. "How soon until we have to decide?"

"Before we leave here, I'm afraid. We've literally reached a fork in the road." he said, studying Mary, who failed to notice him twirling his fork for levity.

"Options?" Mary inquired, staring down at her plate.

"The shortest route into Montana is due north from here. Or we can go west a ways and then turn north. Second choice puts us in the neighborhood of Yellowstone," he stated, knowing that she had mentioned it as a potential destination.

"How close are we?" she asked, taking another large bite despite no longer feeling hungry.

"An hour from the border, if we head due north."

She swallowed hard.

"That close?" Mary replied, not realizing they had actually gotten this far. She turned to see Jesus watching her.

"There are no wrong choices here," he offered, in the way of encouragement.

Emboldened, she decided. "West. We keep going west."

38 – Buffalo, Wyoming

"Is this Yellowstone off to our left?" James asked.

Mary consulted her phone and after some bandwidth latency, she concluded it was not.

"Big Horn National Forest."

They carried on for another five minutes before signs for the national forest confirmed Mary's assessment. Ten more minutes passed before signs for Buffalo, Wyoming appeared.

"Wonder how it got its name?" James asked sarcastically.

"Ha! You're wrong. It's named after Buffalo, New York," she said, referencing her phone again.

"Really?"

"No, I lied," Mary said, laughing. "But I wonder how Buffalo, New York, got its name. Doubt they named it after the animal," she continued, suddenly chasing her mental butterflies once again.

Moments later, they were edging slowly into the small town.

"Buffalo, New York wasn't named after the animal, but after the Buffalo Creek," she said, consulting her phone.

"What would we do without our phones?"

"Probably read a book," Mary answered, pocketing her phone. "Like social media, it would probably be a good thing if we didn't spend so much time on these infernal things."

She had been trying, unsuccessfully, for months to break her own addiction. It should have been easy on this trip, she thought, when you might have God riding shotgun with you.

She was probably stalling for time, but she asked her brother, anyway. "Mind if we cut through town and get out for a while?"

If he suspected her reasons, he didn't let on. He almost seemed too eager, leading her to wonder if he wasn't experiencing the same anxiety she was, as they closed in on the finish line.

Even with the large RV, it wasn't difficult for James to find a parking spot right on Main Street. Above them, a large mural had been painted across a brick building near the corner. The three climbed out and looked up.

A River Runs Through It

"Was that filmed here?" James wondered aloud. "I mean, here's the town and there is a river, literally running through it," he said, pointing.

Mary was reaching for her phone when she caught and then silently chastised herself. Her brother wasn't intrigued enough, at least right now, to bother looking it up himself. And to her knowledge, Jesus didn't even have a phone.

"Isn't this more like a creek?" Jesus clarified, after he stepped across the street.

"You're right," James had to admit, after inspecting it for himself. "What if there was more water running through it, though? Would that make a creek, a river?"

"You think they're going to change all the signs every time it rains?" Mary asked, nodding towards a sign that clearly denoted the waterway as a creek.

"I guess not," James agreed, shaking his head. "Would just be a swollen creek, right?"

Jesus seemed to agree.

Just down the street, James spoke up.

"Hey sis? Step over here and let me take your photo!" he asked.

She decided she'd fulfill his request, posing behind the 'Crazy Woman Square' sign he had found.

"Real cute," Mary said, a wide smile on her face.

The trio then did a quick lap of the town. It didn't take long.

"Without the cars and trucks, and the asphalt pulled up, it probably doesn't look much different now than it had a century ago," Mary noted.

An older gentleman was happening by when he spotted the trio checking out the town and stepped their way, stopping short. An appropriate, socially acceptable distance, left between them and himself.

"You're a few months too early," he said, in way of a greeting, smile on his lips.

"Eguerdion," Jesus said, eliciting an even wider smile from the man, who nodded in appreciation.

"Ongi etorri," he replied.

"Eskerrik asko."

The four of them exchanged looks, the siblings sharing a look of bewilderment.

"What's going on?" James said, leaning over and whispering in her ear.

"I do not know," she replied, her lips not moving.

Jesus and the gentleman laughed.

"Sorry," Jesus said, noting their looks of confusion. "There is a very large Basque population here and they have a festival every year."

"Maybe not this year," the man confided in perfect English, "with everything going on." He looked gravely disappointed.

"Is it soon?" Mary inquired.

"August. We've got the planning down to a science, but we need to sign contracts and extend commitments soon if we're going to pull it off safely this year. I'm on the committee and we're split on pushing it out or canceling it completely this year. We don't have many infections here, thankfully, but people usually come in from all over, and our medical facilities really don't have the capacity for that sort of thing. Don't want to tempt fate, you might say."

"I didn't know that the Basque population in the US was that large? But truthfully, I didn't know that the Basque population in Europe was even that big; no offense," Mary admitted.

The man laughed. "Most people don't even know what Basque represents or that we exist, so I applaud you for even knowing about us. There are probably a couple million Basque living around the world. We might not be that great in numbers, but we make up for it with our zeal in maintaining our heritage. Even have our own chapter here in town."

"What would the area offer?" James asked, not knowing exactly who the Basque were but would ask Mary about it later.

"It's a beautiful area, don't get me wrong. For our first ancestors choosing to settle here, it might have been memories of home. The land looks similar. But it's not so much an attraction as it is a cultural lifestyle. The Basque are explorers by nature."

"Well, thank you," Mary replied, as the man nodded and turned to leave. One last thought coming to mind, he turned back and said, "We'd love to have you come for the festival, but I'd call first."

With practiced ease, he slowed, checking the path in front of him before tripping over any of the bronze statues mounted on the street corner. It was a good thing he did, having stopped only inches away from one of the sheep at his hip. Petting it like a pet, he smiled at the trio. "I swear these things move around more than the real things. Have to watch your step," he said, laughing at some kind of inside joke before disappearing around the street corner.

39 – Sheridan, Wyoming

Time was running out, Mary thought to herself, as they continued north, signs and billboards for Montana becoming more frequent. She literally had what could be the King of Kings, riding along with them on their cross-country adventure, and Mary felt like she was squandering the opportunity.

When they topped one of the rolling hills, they could see both lanes ahead were a sea of red lights. The Winnebago, along with all the other traffic around them, slowed.

Mary took it as a sign and jumped into action, taking off her seatbelt and sliding into the back of the RV to join Jesus on the couch. As always, he greeted her with a smile and nod, not looking surprised at all by her appearance across from him.

When Jesus looked out, noticing that they had exited the interstate, Mary waved dismissively.

"Don't worry, he does this all the time. James would rather spend thirty minutes driving around the backup than idle along for ten minutes to get through it."

"I heard that!" James called out. "Just taking a shortcut, which might be a little longer, and take a few extra minutes."

"I've heard that one before," Mary said with a laugh. With Jesus now giving her his undivided attention again, but not saying anything, she dove right in. "What's heaven like?"

"It's a wonderful place. Your parents are in expert hands."

She nodded, trying to keep herself in the moment. Mary did not know how long Jesus would be around, but was too afraid to ask.

"Thank you for that," she said, not knowing if it was for his sentiment or for arranging it. The bottled-up feelings inside her were all clamoring for attention.

"You're welcome."

"So, if it's not people floating on clouds playing harps, what's it like?"

They both smiled and laughed, picturing the stereotype that was prevalent with so many folks.

"Why do you ask?"

Mary shrugged, clearly not having a reason in mind. "Just curious," she said. "The Bible doesn't say much about it."

"Well, the authors hadn't experienced it yet," he said, in way of an explanation.

That was true, she thought to herself. Can't fault him for that one. "Excellent point."

"But in reality, heaven means different things to different people."

"Pets are allowed, though, right?"

"Wouldn't be heaven without them," he reassured her.

Traffic was backed up at the major intersection in town, as other vehicles from the interstate were also trying out the same 'shortcut' that James had found.

"We should have stayed on the highway," Mary said.

"I heard that too," James noted without turning around.

"That's because I shouted it," she teased.

As the RV rolled up to the light, a small knot of people brandishing signs relating to COVID, came into view on the corner. A few pedestrians who shared the same sidewalk flowed past the five as though they were invisible. Which Mary found hard to believe because each, in some fashion, was decked out in a way that would draw attention anywhere, especially here. And not just because all five were socially distant and wearing masks. Good for them, she noted.

Jesus, looking animated now, reached up and slid the side window open just as the light changed.

"God loves each of you!" he yelled out to them. "I love you too!"

The five turned, all of them so used to not being acknowledged, that the sentiment caught each off guard. Although there was no way to know for sure, unless Mary got out and asked them directly, the rainbow colors and messaging on their signs made her think that at least a few of the LGBTQ acronyms were represented. The individual closest to the RV motioned towards themselves, questioning if Jesus had been referring to them.

"Yes, you. All of you," he clarified, face up to the screen.

The small group smiled, waving goodbye to the RV, as it turned the corner and pulled away.

"That was a beautiful gesture," Mary commented, wondering why she hadn't thought of doing the same thing. Speaking life into people was such a rewarding thing to do, and it literally cost nothing. Why so many people were more likely to tear others down instead of building them up escaped her. Just don't say anything, the old idiom went. Too much energy spent on hate, she thought.

"Must get a lot of grief living here," James said from the driver's seat.

"Not just here, James," Mary noted. "But you're right, there are probably states and cities that are more open to folks living their true, unconventional lives."

"I don't get it. Why not just try to blend in more?"

Mary looked at Jesus, who was watching her intently, that familiar twinkle in his eye.

"They could, but they wouldn't be living authentically," Mary answered. "But you make a good point," she said, taking a different tack.

"I do?" James asked, surprised.

Mary was speaking to her brother, but was looking directly at Jesus.

"People often make the argument that LGBTQ folks aren't living an authentic life. That they intentionally dress up or act in a way that sets them apart from society. But would you voluntarily do that if you faced criticism, derision, grief, potential physical abuse, or discrimination from your family or the public? Would you risk being fired? Or evicted? Or denied treatment by medical professionals or other service providers, just because you *might* be LGBTQ? In some places, you can't even have a cake baked for a special occasion, simply because the baker doesn't like it and claims religious harm would result."

After several moments, James finally responded. "Can all that really happen in this day and age?"

"Oh yes. Very few places have laws prohibiting any of it, and what laws that are out there is a messy, patchwork mix of regulations that the current administration continues to chip away at," Mary added.

"That doesn't seem right," James concluded, going silent. Mary agreed.

"And imagine what all marginalized groups face with health care. Are they going to be first in line at the hospital if they need a ventilator? Will they be getting the vaccine against COVID first or last? Will drugs be available for their viral infections when they're finally developed? I don't imagine they will. LGBTQ. People of color. Immigrants that might not be here legally. They never seem to catch a break in a system that's weighted heavily against them," she said, before changing direction again. "Will they all be okay?" she asked Jesus, not sure she wanted to know the answer, until he had confirmed it.

"They'll all be fine," Jesus said, smiling.

How long had that group been out there, Mary wondered, looking out the window as though they might still be in view? Their signs had comments on them related to the virus, but had they been 'protesting' on that corner for years, railing against a system stacked against them? Was she any different, moving from cause to cause, providing a voice for those who couldn't speak for themselves? Mary knew she didn't belong to a marginalized group per se, but as a woman, her life wasn't completely without frequent discrimination and the occasional episode of unwanted sexual advances, so at least she thought she could relate.

"Here we go!" James announced from the front as the Winnebago turned sharply and began the labored climb up the entrance ramp back onto US-90. Even at their meager top speed, they still overtook a few trucks on the road that looked awfully familiar.

"Told you," she teased.

"What?" James asked.

"That truck we just passed? We passed it earlier, before the backup," Mary said to Jesus.

"No way. That had to be a different truck," James argued, confident his detour had made-up time.

Mary shook her head and smiled, confident that she was right.

40 – Wyoming/Montana State Line

Mary didn't know what to expect or have a specific destination in mind, but since she had declared at lunch, the route they planned to take into Montana, her mood had shifted from apprehension to motivation.

Up ahead and against all odds, she could see a roadway sign that likely showed they were on the verge of moving into another state. Looking around at the rolling hillside filled with swaying grassland, there was no other sign that they were about to cross an arbitrary border.

The Winnebago was plowing ahead, but Mary felt the deceleration even before her brother had brought it to everyone's attention.

"Think we've got a problem," James declared from the driver's seat, as they struggled to maintain headway on I-90. James threw on the hazard lights as their speed continued to fall and traffic closed in behind them.

"Out of gas?"

"Nope, not unless the gauge found a new place to stick and our tank got punctured," he said. As if on cue, wisps of steam because appeared around the edges of the hood.

Mary could feel frustration set in. They were so close! When she looked up again, the roadway sign she had been watching was gone, only visible now in the side mirror as it drifted away behind them in their wake.

James continued to nurse the gas pedal, trying to keep their headway at a survivable thirty miles an hour. But if an exit didn't come up soon, the narrow shoulder would be their next stop. Mary turned around to face their sole passenger, wondering if he had any magic or words of advice.

"This, technically, is Montana," Jesus noted with an encouraging smile. "You made it."

"He's right. We made it to Montana," her brother concurred, looking over at his sister with a sense of relief and disbelief. She smiled too, but he could see her face was full of doubt. Technically, they were correct, but they hadn't quite met the objective yet.

"Thank you for coming. I wouldn't have made it here without you," Mary replied, reaching out and giving her brother's shoulder a squeeze.

"Yes, you would have. You're not fooling me."

That compliment brought a more sincere smile to her tired face.

Up ahead, the first exit came into view. Not exactly a major metropolis, but at least they could get off the interstate.

"Not much here," James noted, stating the obvious. "Left, or right?"

Mary, studying her phone, didn't find much.

"Can't make it another hundred miles?" she asked, laughing.

"We'll be lucky to make it up to that exit."

"Go west. Turn left at the top of the ramp."

The Winnebago bested James' estimate and kept chugging away as though its little soul knew it was vital to their mission.

There was nothing promising up ahead, laid out below the brilliant, sunny, blue sky, save for cattle guards and green grass, so they pushed on at slower and slower speeds.

"Turn right."

Afraid to come to a complete stop or they might never get going again, he confirmed no traffic was coming before rounding the corner. Stop sign ignored.

"How far?"

"Five miles. The closer we get, the less we'll have to walk," Mary replied, trying to motivate both the driver and the vehicle.

They both watched as the wisps of steam from under the edge of the hood grew thicker.

"Don't think the temperature gauge works either," James said with an incredulous smile.

"Should we stop and let it cool down?"

James was pondering the idea just as signs of civilization appeared in dotted fashion on the horizon. He wasn't too keen on walking in the sultry afternoon and figured another mile probably wouldn't hurt.

"I'll pull over in a minute. Hopefully, there's something up ahead."

Some houses appeared on large lots, bordering one side of the road or the other. Eventually, some smaller lots, off to one side, on what would normally be called city streets, came into view. James let the tiny hamlet drift behind them and stayed on the gas pedal instead.

Jesus stepped up and kept them company as the three stared out the windshield, seeing nothing but nature.

"Maybe we should have stopped back there," James stated, the point moot.

Up ahead, a small road sign appeared.

"'Spear'," Jesus read aloud. "I really dislike those things."

Mary couldn't help but smile when she saw he didn't look pained.

When a wide spot in the road presented itself, James decided it was probably better to stop on their terms and not by circumstance.

Up ahead, an expanse of gravel appeared off to their left. As they got closer and cleared a stand of trees, an extensive building materialized from the haze.

"Only sign of civilization, it looks like," James noted.

There was nothing else here. He swung in and parked in the motel's shadow. A few cars sat outside several rooms, so they knew people had to be around. Shutting down the engine, the world went silent. James and Jesus stepped out and looked around. There was literally nothing else here.

When Mary stepped out, she had her bag slung over her shoulder and the box of their father's ashes cradled in her arms.

"I need a shower and I'm going to get us each a room. Any objections?"

They shook their heads.

She emerged with three keys, which she distributed and then turned back towards the motel.

"Back here. Six P.M. sharp," Mary called out over her shoulder. She was taking charge, and it felt good, even though things appeared to be completely out of control. It was a strange feeling and but she let it go, choosing instead to let the circumstances sweep her along.

Once inside her room, which was pleasant and clean, if slightly musty and dated, she locked the deadbolt, tossed on the chain, dropped everything on the bed, stripped down and climbed into the shower, letting the hot water work its magic.

The days were a blur, so many fresh places and faces to absorb. Not to mention the mix of emotions fighting for her attention. Her father was dead, and he wasn't coming back. Even through the shower, she felt hot tears pouring down her face. Instead of wiping them away, she encouraged them to run. Deep breaths gave way to heavy sobs as she settled slowly to the bottom of the tub and cried, the water continuing to rain down.

41 – Spear, Montana

James and Jesus were early, checking out the Winnebago.

"Going to need a tow," James conceded. Jesus nodded in agreement. They both looked up and thought they saw Mary coming their way, but it wasn't the same woman who had wearily wandered off earlier. This person, wearing a beautiful floral summer dress and flats, crossed the road and approached, carrying both their father's ashes and an air of confidence.

"You look amazing," Jesus commented.

Mary blushed, feeling terribly over-dressed.

"Clean up pretty well there, sis."

"Thank you both," Mary acknowledged, trying to keep her plan alive. It had come together in her brain while wallowing in the shower, but out here, it was seeming like folly. She needed to strike while the iron was hot.

They watched her expectantly, wondering what she had in mind.

"The RV?" she asked first, nodding towards the white elephant in the room.

"We'll have to get it towed somewhere tomorrow," James said, shaking his head. "Might start in the morning, but I don't think so."

She nodded. The last pieces were all falling into place. Mary held up their father's box as the men looked at her expectantly.

"Please come with me? There is a stream behind you, relatively close, and it looks like a great place to see dad off," Mary said, through pangs of doubt.

There was a pause as the pair of men exchanged glances, looked behind them, and then turned back to her.

"Sounds like a great idea," James concluded. "Lead the way."

The pair followed her lead and in a couple of minutes; they had worked their way across the field and emerged into a beautiful clearing, a small stream winding its way through a patch of trees. It was perfect and everything she had hoped it would be after finding the spot on her phone earlier.

"Wow," James commented, summarizing the impressions of all of them.

Mary nodded, speechless. She kneeled down at the water's edge and opened the decorative box, exposing a simple, clear, plastic bag inside.

"Think this is legal on tribal land?" James pondered aloud, taking a quick look around. They might as well have been at the end of the world, as remote as the spot felt. He couldn't believe they were only fifty yards from the road and the motel.

"I suspect it's probably illegal everywhere," she concluded, lifting the bag and holding it out to her brother. "Would you do the honors, James?"

He wasn't exactly looking forward to this, but he took the bag and cradled it in his hands in what he hoped looked reverent. "An entire life reduced to rubble," he noted, the weight pressing into his palms. He didn't know if it was his imagination, but it felt heavier than he remembered from Mt. Rushmore.

"Not true. The best parts are already home, James. That's just the broken-down shell remaining in your hands. Not to mention you two, carrying on the legacy of your father through your memories and actions," Jesus reminded him.

James made to reply, but he choked up, unable to speak. He just nodded, either in agreement or simply acknowledging the sentiment. Even Mary felt the tears come again, hoping she had used them up earlier in the shower. Her brother, not sure what to do now, began to undo the wire tie. "Should we say something?" he inquired, looking at Mary.

She nodded, pulled out her phone, found her bookmark, and spoke.

"You're shattered
Like you've never been before
The life you knew
In a thousand pieces on the floor
And words fall short in times like these
When this world drives you to your knees,
You think you're never gonna get back
To the you that used to be
Tell your heart to beat again
Close your eyes and breathe it in
Let the shadows fall away
Step into the light of grace
Yesterday's a closing door
You don't live there anymore
Say goodbye to where you've been
And tell your heart to beat again
Just let those words wash over you
It's alright now
Love's healing hands have pulled you through
So, get back up, take step one
Leave the darkness, feel the sun
'Cause your story's far from over
And your journey's just begun
Tell your heart to beat again"

"First Corinthians?" James asked.

"Danny Gokey," Mary replied. "It stayed with me when mom died."

"Inspiring," Jesus said, nodding and smiling.

James caught her eye and lifted the bag again, silently asking if it was time.

"Not yet. I'm sorry, but I don't have it memorized." She said, looking sheepishly from her phone to Jesus.

"That's why the Father had it written," he said, kneeling beside her at the stream's edge.

"Here it is."

"Praise the Lord.
Praise the Lord, my soul.
I will praise the Lord all my life;
I will sing praise to my God as long as I live.
Do not put your trust in princes,
in human beings, who cannot save.
When their spirit departs, they return to the ground;
on that very day, their plans come to nothing.
Blessed are those whose help is the God of Jacob,
whose hope is in the Lord their God.
He is the Maker of heaven and earth,
the sea, and everything in them
he remains faithful forever."

Mary's voice faltered, choked with emotion, struggling to continue.

Jesus leaned sideways, shoulder touching hers, and continued from memory, eyes turning skyward.

> "He upholds the cause of the oppressed
> and gives food to the hungry.
> The Lord sets prisoners free,
> the Lord gives sight to the blind,
> the Lord lifts up those who are bowed down,
> the Lord loves the righteous.
> The Lord watches over the foreigner
> and sustains the fatherless and the widow,
> but he frustrates the ways of the wicked.
> The Lord reigns forever,
> your God, O Zion, for all generations.
> Praise the Lord."

"Amen!" Jesus added. "That psalm really doesn't get used in many eulogies. It's a shame because it's one of my favorites."

"Amen," both Mary and James added.

Mary looked to Jesus, pleading, if he might select a few chosen words to add. In her eyes, he could see the humble request.

"I have fought the good fight, I have finished the race, I have kept the faith," he said. "Timothy sure had a way with words."

Mary loved it. It was as equally applicable to their own mission than to their father's life.

"Now?" James asked, looking at his sister for approval.

Mary turned to her brother and nodded.

James undid the twist-tie, steeled himself, and leaned forward.

"Goodbye dad," he croaked, no longer trying to stem the flow of tears. Mary wrapped a supportive arm around him, her head leaning against his shoulder. Together, they held the bag out and let its contents slowly spill out.

The heavier particles fell into the water, sounding like a rainstorm. The loose dust, however, carried on a brisk breeze, swirled the powder around them. They both jumped back, holding their breaths and waving their arms in futile defense, as though an invisible, angry wasp horde were after them.

Mary and James stepped further back from the water, brushing at their heads and arms, finally feeling safe to take a cautious breath.

"That happens more often than you would think," Jesus said, chagrinned. "I should probably have warned you."

James nodded in agreement, pulling an unknown bit from his mouth and eyeing it suspiciously.

"One final thought," Jesus began. "Praetereo fini tempori in cello pace."

He shook both their hands tenderly, bowed, nodded, smiled, and walked back towards the RV and the motel.

"Are you leaving now?" Mary asked, a sense of panic and loss striking her again with a power she hadn't expected.

"Mission accomplished," Jesus said simply, taking them both in one last time.

"Our mission? Or yours?" James inquired quietly.

"Both," he said. "Don't forget that I'm always with you." With that, he turned and walked away, disappearing through the trees in seconds and was gone for a second time.

Mary didn't want Jesus to get away so quickly, so she snatched up the box from the grass and ran to catch him, her brother in tow. As they rounded the clump of trees, visibility clear in all directions for thirty yards, Jesus was nowhere to be seen. He had simply vanished.

"How does he do that?" James asked, but Mary had no answer.

They gave up looking for him and did the only plausible thing; they returned to civilization.

James first checked the door of the Winnebago and confirmed it was locked. He took a quick peek inside the small compartment in the back of the Winnebago to confirm that it, too, was empty and secured it again.

"What do you keep looking for in there?" she asked, still puzzled.

James shook his head as though it were nothing and together, they returned to their respective rooms.

While James showered and changed before they ate dinner, Mary returned to her room and flopped on the bed, a sense of peace and accomplishment finally displacing her fear and apprehension. They had completed the last task that their father had given them and they had done it together. In the end, it had happened just as she had envisioned it. Maybe not in the exact location she would have selected, but it had worked out fine.

She reached over and turned on the television, not caring what came on, in order to kill some time and take her mind off of everything, even for a few minutes.

"Moscow's not the worry, neither is the whole Soviet Navy. I know their tactics; I have the advantage. The worry is the Americans," Sean Connery said to his worried second-in-command, played by Sam Neill.

Hunt for Red October. One of dad's favorite movies, she remembered. He had watched it often while she was over at his house, but Mary was usually toiling around space helping him out with chores after mom had passed away. She should have sat down with him more often, she thought, a wave of loss and guilt threatening to strike again. She moved to grab the remote, but something in the back of her mind stayed her hand.

Bang. Bang. Bang.

"Gunfire?"

"That's what it sounded like, sir."

"He won't change his mind, huh, Ryan?"

"It's gotta be one of the crew."

"Well, whoever he is, I'd say he's having second thoughts."

Mary searched her memory, but this part of the movie didn't sound familiar to her. She watched as Sam Neill's character, Captain Borodin, slumped to the deck, eyes wide, blood oozing from the center of his chest.

"Oh no!" Mary exclaimed, moving to the edge of the bed, riveted. "Not Sam Neill!" He was one of her favorites.

Fully engrossed in the drama playing out in front of her, she kicked up the volume a few notches.

With his life leaking away, Sam Neill looked up at Sean Connery, resignation clear on his face, and uttered his last words.

"I would have liked to have seen Montana."

Mary felt like someone had just kicked her.

"What did he just say?" she asked herself, a wave of panic washing over her, face suddenly beading with sweat. She hadn't heard it right, did she? She snatched at the remote, looking for a pause button or a reverse, but it didn't have any of those features.

Nauseous, she let the quote drift through her mind, examining every single word.

"I would have liked to have seen Montana." she repeated in her head. Mary could even picture her father, accent included, tossing that quote out casually to the nurse as he drew his final breath, laughing at the absurdity of it all.

"Oh. My. God!"

She threw down the remote, leaped to her feet, grabbed several items from the room and rushed to the door, throwing it open. Dashing to the room right next to hers, she began banging frantically on it until her brother, wrapped in the less than luxurious motel robe and slippers, finally answered.

42 – Spear, Montana

Mary and James were on their knees next to the stream. She had lost both shoes running across the field and his robe, which had caught and torn on a branch, hung disheveled across his lanky frame as they peered down at the water's edge. Each had their room's respective trash can in one hand and were wielding the laminated television channel card from their rooms to scrape up whatever looked like the dusty remains of their father from the sand and water's edge.

"Finding anything?" she asked frantically, still winded from the sprint from the motel, hair hanging down as she studied the ground and water only inches below her nose.

"I'm not sure," he replied, erring on the side of caution and sweeping sand, twigs, and small stones into the trash can.

"I can't believe we brought him here. We don't even know if he's ever even been in this state."

James was the first to recognize the futility of their efforts, most of their father probably in the next county by now. He first looked at this sister, who was still straining and scraping at the earth, and then at the peaceful surroundings. Dappled sunlight rained down from a beautiful, blue sky only broken by an occasional fluffy, white cloud. A gentle breeze came down the narrow channel, swirling the canopy of trees above them.

James knew it wasn't a topic that he had ever given much thought to, but when he died, this wouldn't be such an awful place to end up, he concluded.

"Why did you stop?" Mary inquired, noticing him take a break out of the corner of her eye. When he didn't answer, she paused and then she too rocked back on her heels and studied him with a questioning glance.

James turned to his sister and shook his head, a smile on his face. "I think dad would approve of us leaving him here, particularly since we did it together."

Mary thought her brother looked at peace, then looked on as he took his waste bin, leaned it out over the water's edge and held it there, watching and waiting for Mary to react.

Like him, she appraised the area with fresh eyes and reached the same conclusion. Standing up and joining her brother, they each turned their containers in unison, letting the contents spill back into the water, the silky cloud quickly washing away downstream.

"Let's go get a drink," she said, walking gingerly back towards the motel, searching for her missing shoes.

"Can I get dressed first?" he asked, trying unsuccessfully to secure what was left of his robe and his dignity.

Epilogue, Maryvillle, MO

The faded, gray strip of asphalt, labeled on Google Maps as US-71, carried the Winnebago east this time, under a dazzling noon-day sun. Herds of cattle lined the fences, watching them as they crossed the grassy countryside.

"Hungry?" James asked. Some kind of truck stop advertised ahead.

Mary nodded.

They chose a booth up front with a view of the parking lot and sat down.

On their travels, and especially when they stopped, Mary watched the world, hoping to spot Jesus once again.

James knew who she was looking for, but said nothing, because he often did the same thing. Life seemed a little less magical without their dining companion with them, he admitted to himself. Funny how quickly he had become a part of their family.

They basked in the sun's glow as it spilled in the large front windows.

"Would you like me to close the shades?" the server asked.

"No, thank you," James replied, before Mary had a chance. She smiled at him, clearly in agreement with his decision.

"What can I get you?" The young man asked, taking out the tiny carbon pad that seemed prevalent wherever they ate.

"Blueberry pancakes," James answered, no alterations. "And orange juice."

"Ma'am?"

"Tenderloin sandwich, fries, and a Diet Pepsi."

"Diet Coke, okay?" the young man clarified.

"Of course," she replied, forgetting she wasn't at home.

After the server stepped away, James leaned forward, eyes searching the immediate area, and then spoke in a conspiratorial whisper.

"What's wrong with the hamburger here?"

She laughed heartily, drawing attention from everyone in the room, and James joined her. It felt good.

"Nothing. I'm sure they're fine. I just felt like a change was in order."

The food arrived, and neither was disappointed.

"Marvelous." James said.

"I agree."

They continued eating and making small talk until both their plates and their conversation thinned out.

"What's next for you, sis? Back to the picket line?"

"Not for the old cause," she said. "Might have to rethink some things once we get home. Have to find a new job if the old one doesn't open back up soon. Unlike the millions of dollars you're about to find, my bank account is getting a little lean. I'm very happy that we did this, don't get me wrong, but financially, it might not have been the best idea."

"Yeah, me too. Hopefully, a second surge doesn't derail a return to a new normal. I'm in the same boat. Not much coming in for contract work right now, and when things start up again, there's going to be a lot more competition," James admitted. "Hopefully, we all won't get out of this without learning a few lessons."

It impressed Mary, noting a change that had been developing in her brother.

"And that no matter what happens, we shouldn't forget to count our blessings and be thankful for what we have, and not what we don't. It can all be taken away in an instant," she reminded him.

"Jesus always provides," James added.

"Amen," she said, as their server approached.

"Do we pay up front?" James asked, taking the bill.

"Yes, sir."

James moved to take out the cash as Mary finished the last of her fries. He noticed the lottery ticket he had purchased just over a week ago. His hand drew it out, a flicker over the lunch counter catching his eye. The news program had just cut away. Instead of the usual commercials, though, the multi-state lottery numbers appeared on the screen, many of which looked vaguely familiar. He looked at the screen and then down at his hand. Back to the screen, then down to his hand again.

"What's wrong?" Mary asked, suddenly concerned by the change that had come over James.

"Can you check these please?" he asked, passing her the ticket, a slight tremble in his hand.

"Sure," she replied with a smile, unsure of why he was asking.

Mary removed her phone and took a moment to find the website. She swiped through the various games and located the correct set of numbers, comparing them to what was printed on the waxy square of paper in her hand.

James watched her, the amusement on her face turning momentarily to confusion as her eyes looked from phone to ticket and back again. Her eyes widened and mouth hung open as the realization struck home. Apparently, James noted, he had been correct.

She looked up at him and smiled. "Oh my God!" Mary exclaimed, fighting to contain a scream.

"Exactly," James replied, breathless.

From the shadows between two parked tractor trailers, Jesus watched his friends in celebration, knowing they were going to be alright.

The driver of one of the rigs, who had offered Jesus a ride, approached from the truck stop, two coffees in his hand.

"You good?" The man asked, noticing the tears in Jesus' eyes and wide smile on his face.

"Perfect."

Made in the USA
Middletown, DE
06 September 2022

72509390R00221